THE CHOSEN ONE

A SOLDIER OF LIGHT NOVEL - BOOK ONE

Be the light
Ashley ♡

THE CHOSEN ONE

A SOLDIER OF LIGHT NOVEL
- BOOK ONE -

ASHLEY LEBLANC

 FriesenPress

One Printers Way
Altona, MB R0G 0B0
Canada

www.friesenpress.com

ISBN
978-1-03-918481-7 (Hardcover)
978-1-03-918480-0 (Paperback)
978-1-03-918482-4 (eBook)

1. FICTION, VISIONARY & METAPHYSICAL

Distributed to the trade by The Ingram Book Company

For

Everyone who didn't think they could and did

Those that haven't and will

And

Whoever loves a Good Story

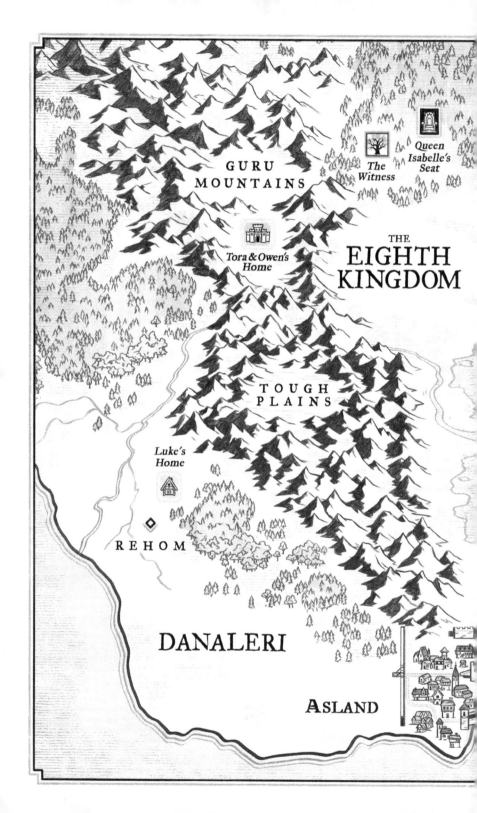

ONE

 King Nadiri stumbled on a low, protruding rock, stubbing his toe and pitching forward. With a yelp, he reached out, looking to break his fall, and grabbed the hanging roots to his left. Despite how slick they were in the driving rain, he was able to find purchase, stopping his fall before he did a face-plant in the mud. As he pulled himself upright, his generals watched with concern. Only then did Nadiri realize the roots were a curtain covering the mouth of a cave, which he would have missed if he hadn't stumbled. The cave mouth was three times his height and double that wide. Shaking his head working to clear the haze of exhaustion and defeat, he used his sword to slash a rough opening for himself and his men.

They had been forced to make a hasty retreat—again—leaving behind their wounded and anything that had been stuck in the quagmire of muck that was known as Pacihalla. Rule number one: anyone who was wounded and couldn't retreat was left behind. However, Nadiri wondered if he ever did win a battle, would he want to treat the wounded? If a man couldn't fight, what good was he? Shaking his head, rain flying out from his dripping hair, he brought his mind back to the task at hand.

He had decided to attack Pacihalla, knowing it held a heavy risk but a great reward should he prevail, which had allowed his army to be lured into the bog and dispatched immediately. Nadiri knew he had been defeated—again—as he watched the front ranks of his army sink into the bog, so he decided to cut his losses. As he was trying to make his hasty retreat with his top generals, the enemy had flanked them and attacked from the rear. Nadiri barely made it out alive, and the generals who survived only did so due to their exceptional fighting ability and experience.

"Jensen, Harley, with me," he said as he entered the cave. "The rest of you, stay here." The two generals followed him into the cave, hacking and slashing at the roots that barred their way.

As they stepped over the threshold, they saw stalactites hanging from the ceiling. Oddly, a torch was burning on the wall, as if they had been expected. Jensen plucked it out of the bracket, then handed it to Nadiri as he made his way deeper into the cave. When they had determined the cave was unoccupied, Nadiri sent Jensen back to bring the other men to rest and regroup.

While what was left of his army got settled, Nadiri explored deeper into the cave, walking around a bend that couldn't be seen from the opening. Normally, he wouldn't have bothered, but he felt something pulling him deeper. When he rounded the bend, he found the source of the call.

Leaning against a rock was a broad sword in a scabbard. The scabbard was wrought with symbols he didn't recognize, etched into the midnight-black leather. The ornate hilt looked as if the devil himself had designed it. Between the cross guard and pommel was the sculpture of a demon's face. The long, curving horns growing out of its head, huge fangs, and dead, hollow eyes made it seem as if it were watching Nadiri's every step. He prided himself on never being scared or weak, but this sword sent fear down his spine and into his bowels.

Taking another tentative step toward the devil's sword, he noticed writing on the grip. He tipped his head sideways to read it. *Taker. Taker? Taker of what? Lives for sure,* Nadiri thought. The pommel was inset with a black diamond that seemed to be a counterbalance to the sword. Nadiri approached the weapon with caution, wondering if he was delirious. He wasn't sure, but it looked like the scabbard was swallowing the light from his torch, drawing him closer, as if he were in a trance.

Unable to control himself, Nadiri reached out and drew the sword from its scabbard. As soon as the blade was exposed—the first time in the Earth dimension since its inception—the smell of brimstone tickled Nadiri's nose. Then two things happened almost simultaneously. As the weak light touched the matte-black blade, a black, greasy wave of energy crawled along the ground, covering every dark corner of the cave and beyond.

The second thing occurred in a cave not unlike the one the king was in, only this second cave was on the other side of the continent. The egg-size, crystal-clear diamond in the pommel of a second sword exploded with an eternal light, sending it down the sword, which was called Light Bringer, and making its blade radiant, like lightning. For an instant, the intensity of the light turned night into day before it disappeared as an orb, finding a new home in the love of two great people.

By the time the first sword, Light Taker, found freedom, a black wave of light was creeping across the ground, out of the cave, and across Nadiri's kingdom.

The matte-black blade had silver symbols etched toward the hilt. As Nadiri held the blade up to his torch, the sword sucked in the light and swallowed it. After careful inspection, Nadiri realized the symbols were the same as the ones on the scabbard.

Nadiri had no idea where the sword came from, but somehow he knew it had been left there for him. Replacing the sword in the scabbard and throwing the baldric over his shoulder, he noted the sword rested perfectly on his hip, as if it had been fitted for him. He also noticed his torch was lighting the whole area again.

Interesting, Nadiri thought. Shaking his head, he made his way back to his men, so they could assess the damage and decide on their next move.

TWO

The Seven Kingdoms had never been united—until now. Many had tried, bringing war to their neighbors' doorsteps, but all had failed. King Gurham had, at last, completed the work his grandfather started. The problem had been that each kingdom was prosperous unto itself, not needing its neighbors. However, through open communication and holding back food until the heads of state agreed (a dirty but effective tactic), Gurham had achieved peace in his kingdom. Little did he know his timing couldn't have been more perfect.

King Gurham stood at the window of his chamber watching flakes of snow drift to the ground in the twilight. He had been working for decades to unite the Seven Kingdoms, and his dream was about to come to fruition. He was excited at the prospect of creating a positive legacy for his children. He didn't do it because he wanted more subjects or a bigger army. He did it because it was the right thing to do and because he was the right man for the job. If he had his way, he would take his queen and build a hut in the woods to live in tranquility and peace. Unfortunately, that was not his path in this lifetime. He had come to terms with his role early in life and had thrown himself into being a just and fair king, earning the loyalty of his subjects.

He strode to his desk and smiled at the pile of treaties spread across its surface. Sitting, he pulled one off the top and was about to start reading it when he heard the door to his chamber open. Turning in his chair, his breath caught. His best friend, confidant, and lover, Queen Shanti, strode into the room. Her wavy, raven-black hair tumbled down her straight back to her slim waist. A green jewel sparkled at her throat, a gift from her king, bringing out her purple eyes and matching her low-cut gown, her breasts almost spilling out. Maintaining eye contact, she tugged at the strings of her gown, loosening the bindings of her corset. It landed in an emerald pool around her feet. Stepping out of it, she peeled off her undergarments one by one, gliding toward her king as if magnetically pulled to him. Now naked, she straddled him, settling on his lap. She looked deep into his eyes, and when she could stand it no longer, she brought her lips to his. They could feel their ladinya, the life essence of all, intertwining, the two becoming one. The world was just them and their love. She gave herself to him, and he gave himself to her.

He wrapped his arm around her waist and carried her to their bed. Then he set her on her feet beside the bed, stepping back to indulge in her beauty, healthy and curvaceous in her strength. When he couldn't stand it any longer, he pulled off his pants and boots and shucked his shirt, the queen laughing at the speed of his actions. He removed his undergarments and pulled her naked body against his. When her bare breasts pressed against the soft hair of his chest, he noticed they were swollen and tried to think if it was her moon time. He must have been thinking too hard because the queen giggled and placed a hand on his face.

"Where did you go, my king?" Her voice washed over him like water to a man dying of thirst.

He chuckled. "I noticed your breasts are looking swollen—and fantastic—and I was trying to do the math to determine if it's your moon time."

"Oh! No, no, it's not," she replied, a little surprised. It amazed her how well he knew her and how attentive he was.

Lying on the bed, she pulled him on top of her, no space

between their bodies, minds, or souls. He slid into her, and she pulled him deeper with her legs until he could go no further. Then they danced the oldest dance, climaxing together.

The king and queen lay like entwined lovers, satiated and fulfilled. She stroked his head, which was lying on her chest, as she felt him relax into a deep sleep. The weight of his body and the rhythm of his breath was the lullaby she needed to drift off to dreamland.

Sometime later, an ember of light intentionally floated into the room on the moonbeam that was shining across their slumbering bodies. The ember hovered for a moment, watching the figures in the bed and assessing whether this was the right choice. Just then, the queen rolled onto her side, the king unconsciously pulling her against him, sharing his heat. Neither of them woke up.

In the queen's womb, as the result of their lovemaking, two became one. Then one became two, and two became four. The ember decided this was the right path. Traveling through the king's hand on the queen's belly, it found its new home.

THREE

Queen Shanti paced around her private bedchamber, wringing her hands.

"What does it feel like?" a soothing voice asked, causing Shanti to pause in the afternoon sunlight beaming through the windows. She looked into the green eyes of her best friend and healer, Ari. "Tainted. Like I'm dirty and can't get clean."

Looking at the regal queen of the Seven Kingdoms, one wouldn't think she knew what getting dirty meant. She wore a deep purple gown with a sweetheart neckline and an empire waist, using her growing belly as a fashion statement. She wore it because it was comfortable, and she liked the color. She looked nothing like the hard-working farm girl she had been growing up. Her strong spirit and her independent nature were two of her best qualities, in her husband's opinion.

Ari's brow furrowed in thought. "That's a pretty specific feeling. How long have you been feeling this?" she asked, her eyes trailing the queen as she began pacing again.

"Mmmm... a few days. It crept up so slowly I couldn't tell you exactly."

"Would you like me to take a look?"

"Could you? I don't know what to think."

"It would be my pleasure." Ari bowed her head and smiled. "Lie on the table." She pointed to a padded table in an alcove tucked into the corner of the room.

The queen laid on her back, Ari arranging pillows under her

knees. Queen Shanti was about five moons along, so she was still comfortable lying on her back. Ari draped a blanket over her and then folded down the top, which allowed Ari to place her hand on the queen's exposed chest, over her heart. She placed her other hand on Queen Shanti's forehead. "Breathe. In... two... three... four. Hold... two... three... four. And out... two... three... four. Hold out... two... three... four." The Calming Breath was how they started every treatment, and Queen Shanti had received hundreds.

Ari's voice was a lullaby, rocking the queen into total relaxation. When Queen Shanti was breathing steadily on her own, Ari closed her eyes and bowed her head.

In her mind's eye, she was standing in a dimly lit cavern. A large, leather-bound book lay atop a gold-veined marble altar standing in the center and illuminating the area. Attached to the altar were countless ribbons that were anchored to the cavern walls all around. There were ribbons of every color and size and in every condition, and they all had writing on them in different colored inks. Some had fallen from where they had broken, draped over the ones below. A few had crumbled to dust, and Ari knew they would completely disintegrate if she touched them, though she would not dare. Ari wandered through them, keeping an eye out for something that didn't belong. She had walked about halfway around when she saw it.

An ominous dark cloud swirled around a unique ribbon. It was anchored to the wall and the altar just like the others. Except it wasn't just like the others. As Ari approached cautiously, she saw light blinking under the nefarious, churning black cloud, trying to hide the light. She stopped when a face appeared in the cloud. It opened its mouth to speak, but Ari cut it off.

"Who are you?"

The entity squinted at Ari in annoyance. Agents of darkness

liked to have the first word, which Ari knew.

"He said you would ask," the cloud replied, his voice grating against Ari's senses, making her cringe.

"Uh-huh. Who sent you?"

"That's for me to know and you to find out."

"Obviously. That's why I asked," Ari snapped, her patience wearing thin.

"I don't see what he sees in you," the cloud grumbled, unhappy with his assignment.

"Zion," Ari hissed. *OK, this guy needs to go.* "Are you going to leave of your own volition?"

"No!"

"Last chance. Are you going to leave?" Ari's voice rang through the cavern.

"No!"

Taking a deep breath, she focused on the cloud as a ball of white light appeared in her right hand. She moved the fingers of her left hand, which she held out in front of her, causing the cloud to loosen its grip on the ribbon of light and collect in a ball above it. The roiling black cloud screamed in protest, whipping out tendrils and trying to wrap them around the light ribbon. Ari peeled the tendrils from the ribbon, collecting them in a ball and holding them in the prison of light with her intention.

"You do not belong here!" she proclaimed. "You do not have a purpose here. You are not needed here. BE GONE INTO THE LIGHT!"

Her voice thundered through Queen Shanti's bedchamber as the entity flew from the queen's chest to the air above her. Ari was ready. She wrapped it in the light she had in her right hand, saturating the black cloud with ethereal light. When it couldn't hold one more iota, it exploded, embers floating through the air and dispersing into the ether, creating a beautiful light show.

"What was that?" Queen Shanti asked, propping herself up on her elbows.

"A saboteur. Lie down, and I'll double check that it's all gone. Then we can have a talk." Queen Shanti lowered herself onto her back and resumed her steady breathing.

Ari closed her eyes. Once again she was in the cavern. She gingerly walked over to the ribbon of light, noting the gold writing. It looked sturdy, sure, and undamaged. Noting that everything appeared to be back to normal, she came out of her mind's eye and looked down at the queen.

"That's everything for today. You can sit up when you're ready. Take your time." Queen Shanti gently moved her body, bringing life back to her limbs.

"What did the saboteur want?" Queen Shanti asked.

"It was sent here to sabotage one of your soul agreements." Ari held up her finger to stall the queen's next question while she explained. "Between you and your baby. I found it and released it. Do you still feel tainted?"

"No. Not at all." Queen Shanti sat up, swinging her legs off the side of the table. Standing, she stretched, took a deep breath, and began walking back and forth in front of Ari, who watched her gait for abnormalities.

"Soul agreement?" Queen Shanti prompted.

"When our souls decide to come to Earth, we enlist help from others. It can be as benign as an agreement with the baker, that he will provide food, and you will pay him for his services, or it can be deep and complicated. The one the entity was trying to sabotage was of great importance for all of us."

Shanti stopped pacing and stared at Ari. "Ari, what's going on?" She sounded scared.

"I can't say because I don't know. But it's not worth worrying about. These things happen to everyone. All we can do is regular check-ins and focus on creating a happy, healthy baby. We have other things to talk about that are much more important." Ari wiggled her eyebrows at the queen. "Like a name."

Shanti clasped Ari's hands. "I was hoping you could name him. At the birth."

Ari's eyes teared up. "It would be an honor, my queen." Her voice cracked with emotion, then she dropped into a deep curtsy, one hand lifting the side of her skirt, the other under her chin, her head bowed as she showed the utmost respect.

"Thank you," Queen Shanti replied. As they hugged, Ari felt the baby kick against her stomach where it was pressed against the queen's.

"Apparently, he agrees."

They both broke down laughing.

FOUR

The castle's white marble spires shone in the low sun, flags snapping in the winter wind. It was the last day of a week of great celebration, the shortest day of the year and the full moon. The castle was bustling with activity as staff prepared for the multifaceted celebration. The Seven Kingdoms were finally reunited under one king. King Gurham on his stallion, with Queen Shanti by his side, rode through the city, throwing gold medallions to his subjects. It was a time of prosperity, and he wanted to share it with his people, who deserved it. It was their sacrifices that had motivated his grandfather to unite the Seven Kingdoms for the first time in history. Unfortunately, his grandfather and father had passed before he'd met this goal, but Gurham was more than happy to continue their work.

Uniting the Seven Kingdoms wasn't so much a matter of conquering as it was about coming together to leverage resources. Many trips and meetings had led to this day.

"Are you OK, my queen?" he asked his beloved, reaching for her hand.

"Yes," she replied, taking his hand in hers as she rode beside him, "although I'm ready for quiet time." She blew out a breath as the baby shifted, pressing against her lungs.

He squeezed her hand. "Guards, my queen is weary. Let's go back to the castle, so she can rest before the feast."

The soldiers made a wedge, protecting their king and queen and allowing them to make their way back to the castle in record time. They trotted into the center courtyard. Before his horse came to a complete stop, King Gurham dismounted, then helped Shanti do the same. Normally, he wouldn't have had to help her, as she was an accomplished rider; however, she was hugely swollen with their first child, and he wanted her to take the utmost care.

"Thank you, my king," Queen Shanti said with a deep breath. "I'm going to my chambers to lie down and prepare for this evening's feast."

He lowered his head and cupped her face in his hands, kissing her long and deep. His tongue probed her lips, gently parting them, and his arm wrapped around her waist, pulling her against him, her huge belly pushing into his. After his tongue had explored her mouth and he was satisfied, he broke away, leaving her breathless, the cacophony of activity in the yard around them once again filling their ears. It wasn't unusual to see the king and queen showing such displays of affection.

King Gurham didn't know he could feel love like the love he felt for her. While growing up, he had been told that his first duty was to his kingdom, then to himself. He knew things could be different, and the moment he saw Shanti at the ball where they met, he'd known he could indeed be loyal to both. Now his wife was carrying their first child, and he couldn't have been more excited. They had gotten married with dreams of having a large family, as was customary for royalty, and yet this was her first pregnancy. At least it was going well, after a bit of a rocky start of throwing up in the morning, which had quickly been healed by Ari.

"Do you need assistance, my queen?" Ari inquired as she approached the royal couple.

"Yes, thank you." Shanti took Ari's arm, and they wound their way through the castle.

"How are you feeling?" Ari asked as they made their way up a staircase, the queen waddling beside her.

"Much better since drinking the tonic you gave me. The light healing has helped as well. Thank you for that. I've been having more back pain today, but that could be the huge weight I'm carrying." She paused at the top of the staircase, leaning on Ari to catch her breath.

"It's my pleasure. After all, if I can't help my friends, who can I help?" Ari asked through a smile.

When Ari had found out that Queen Shanti was pregnant with the heir to the Seven Kingdoms, she immediately came to her side, offering her services, expertise, and support.

Ari's cloak swirled around her strong, shapely legs as she steered Shanti toward her chamber. When a gust of wind blew down the corridor, she pulled her hood up to cover her head, which was shaved on both sides.

When they finally reached the royal bedchamber, Ari ordered some tea and food and then helped Queen Shanti settle into bed. She palpated the queen's stomach, making sure the baby was OK.

"Mmmmm…"

"Is that a good 'mmmmm'?" Queen Shanti asked, her head back against the pile of pillows, her eyes closed.

"Yes. Well, he's feeling restless, almost like he's ready to come out any minute. I noticed your belly was dropping down."

"I noticed that, too, though I'm not sure what it means."

"It means he's getting ready to come into the world." Ari's tone was that of a teacher. "He's moving into the birth canal. It's also the Night of the Longest Day, and Sister Moon is known for moving water. Maybe he has things to do in this world that can't wait, making him come early."

Queen Shanti laughed. "Well, he's welcome anytime as long as he's healthy. I can't wait to meet him. We've tried so hard, and he's the biggest blessing in our lives. I know my husband is excited to be a father, to pass on his knowledge and experience."

There was a knock at the door, and a servant entered carrying tea and snacks on a tray. She placed it on the table, then curtsied and left, closing the door behind her.

Ari made tea and a plate of food for the queen, but when she turned back to the bed to serve her, Shanti was asleep, her chin drooping against her chest as she leaned back against the pillows. Ari pulled the blanket up, making sure the queen would be comfortable, then made her leave.

FIVE

Ari was sitting at her mirror ensuring the random strands of her curly hair were tucked into her high bun when there was a knock at her door. Turning, she called for the person to enter.

"The queen asked for you. She is having stomach pains," a dark-haired servant said as she entered the room.

Ari grabbed her medicine bag and swept out of the room, the skirt of her formal gown flapping behind her. She flew down the hall, her slippers silent on the stone. She burst into the royal chamber, the maid following her, and swooped down on Shanti, who was squatting next to the bed holding her belly while trying to breathe.

"What is it, my queen? What's the matter?" She put her hand on Shanti's sweaty brow.

"He's…" She harshly blew out a breath. "Coming!" she screamed as another contraction racked her body. Just then her water broke, soaking the bottom of her nightdress and Ari's skirt and slippers.

"Go get the king, and tell him to hurry," Ari said to the dark-haired servant, who was standing by the door. "His son is almost here." The girl turned and ran from the room.

"I guess he's ready," Queen Shanti said, laughing and sobbing through the pain.

As she paced the room between contractions, Shanti continued to breathe. Ari held her from behind when the contractions gripped Shanti's body, feeding her light to keep the ladinya moving and minimize the pain. Unfortunately, that was all Ari could do. Shanti needed to be able to feel when to breathe and when to push.

"Do you think it's time to lie down?" As soon as the words left Ari's mouth, she heard heels clicking in the hall outside the room. The door opened, and King Gurham strode through the door in his full regalia. It was quite a sight, and Queen Shanti smiled when she saw him.

"What can I do to help?" he asked, taking Shanti in his arms.

"Take her to the bed and sit behind her. Allow her to tell you where to sit, so she can hold on to you. Listen to what she needs, and don't complain about the pain. You can't begin to imagine what she's going through."

Fear fluttered through his heart as he wondered what Ari was talking about, unable to bear seeing his wife in such pain.

Queen Shanti's screams echoed down the corridor and throughout the castle. King Gurham almost cried out in pain when his wife squeezed his hands. Now he understood what Ari was talking about. He was a hardened warrior, and yet he knew if he wasn't careful, his wife would break his hand.

In the midst of the deep moans and high-pitched shrieks that were only heard during childbirth, a high-pitched cry broke through the cacophony. It was a time to rejoice. A new prince had been born. Drenched and exhausted, Shanti watched her little light being as Ari placed him on her chest. He wiggled his body, so his mouth could find her nipple, making Shanti laugh between exhausted sobs as her husband patted her sweaty brow from his spot behind her.

"He's magnificent," King Gurham said, awe seeping from his voice.

The baby had a glow around him as if encased in a golden egg. The glow shimmered when the clouds parted, and a moonbeam stretched across the family. As the baby nursed, the staff cleaned up and then left the new parents to have a quiet moment together with their son. Ari also stepped away, collecting her gear. She was blessed to have witnessed the heir's birth, and she knew she was there not only for her light healing and naming abilities but also for her friendship and support.

When the prince finished nursing, Queen Shanti swaddled him in a blanket and then handed him to Ari. She held the precious package close to her heart, humming a tuneless song while she ambled toward the window to welcome the new life with the rising of the full moon.

As Sister Moon swung through the sky, Earth's water moving with her will, she shone as bright as a second sun, her radiance bathing the city. Every fifty years she blessed the people with eternal day to sweep up the bounty of the sea and rejoice in what she had provided. The whole city helped the fishermen pull nets overflowing with delicacies from the sea, the fishmongers clean the fish, and the cooks prepare the feast, at which they would then sit and be merry. Part of the celebration was a birthday party, as a large portion of the city had been born on that one night. Those people would share their birthday with the new heir.

The moon reached its peak, its silvery light pulling Ari's attention away from the baby's wrinkled brow. Her face bathed in the unearthly glow, she acknowledged the moon's elegant song and then looked down at the miracle in her arms. Touching his brow, she sang in an angelic soprano. "Prince Jaya, the First of His Name, Star Born, Prince of the Seven Kingdoms. I welcome thee from the light." His metallic purple eyes blinked open, focusing on her face. Moon bows from the diamonds covering the top of her gown dappled the space around them in a kaleidoscope of color and light.

The moon was kissing her face when she saw a glimpse into Jaya's future. She was looking through his eyes, the long light

THE CHOSEN ONE 19

in his hand blinding. The light was raised against an unidenti-fied black-shaped foe. She blinked, and the vision passed. Despair clutched her heart as she knew there was a prophecy that this could have partially fulfilled, but she didn't think it was enough until she heard shouting outside the chamber.

Shifting her grasp on Jaya to free one arm, she created an orb of light in her hand as she turned toward the door. A moment later, it burst open, and soldiers in full armor, swords raised, flooded through the door. Well, at least they tried to.

Ari didn't feel scared. She was enraged. Blood red clouded her vision as she prayed for vengeance. A red ball of light in her hand reflected her rage, hissing and spitting like magma spewing from an angry volcano. She was livid that these men would disrupt her friend during such a precious experience, one for which the queen had waited her entire life. She was also angry that she had to step into the role of grim reaper while holding a beautiful new life and furious that her gown would be ruined in the process. Sure, that last detail didn't seem like a big deal, but she hated being wasteful.

As the soldiers poured into the room, swords and armor clanking, Ari moved between the king and queen, who was still in her birthing bed, exhausted. She momentarily calculated the possibilities in her head and knew she couldn't allow the soldiers to get to Jaya or his parents. Once the soldiers decided to hurt her friends, their lives became forfeit.

Using her anger, grief, and joy (at being able to protect Jaya and his parents) as fuel, she focused on the spitting orb of light in her palm, channeling mountain energy. Unmoving, unyield-ing, and defiant, she used the focused energy to send orbs of light through the head of the first soldier, the chest of the second soldier, and the torso of the third. Red mist bloomed in the air, the smell of burned flesh assaulting her nose. She dispatched man after man, efficiency being the key.

When the last soldier came through the door, she blew his legs off, splattering the hallway with blood. He fell on the pile of body parts that Ari had created, blood spurting from the arteries in his legs.

"Who sent you?" Ari demanded as she stood in the pool of his blood, Jaya tucked under her arm and around her breast.

"I'll never…" Pushing himself up on his elbows, he tried taking a stand. Ari bent down and grabbed his collar, pulling him up so they were almost nose to nose.

"WHO SENT YOU?" she demanded, unleashing her wrath, a palpable entity entering the room. The concussion from her focused rage washed over him, pushing the last breath out of his lungs.

"The king… of the eighth…" Before he could say anything more, he died.

This was Not. Good.

Dropping the man, Ari checked on Jaya. He was splattered with blood but appeared to be unhurt. He was asleep, snoring, a stream of drool running from the corner of his rosebud lips. She turned back to the queen and king, whose jaws were hanging open in horror. The entire incident had taken two breaths.

"Did I just see what I think I saw?" Queen Shanti asked. She was so tired she believed she could have imagined the whole thing regardless of the pile of bodies and the pool of viscera in which Ari was standing.

"Yes, my queen." Ari placed Jaya in Shanti's arms, then wiped the spatters of blood from his face. "I'm afraid this doesn't bode well."

"What is it? Ari, tell me." This wasn't Shanti, her good friend, asking; this was Queen Shanti, she who embodied peace and ruled the Seven Kingdoms at King Gurham's side, demanding the truth.

"There is a prophecy, and with this incident"—Ari looked over her shoulder at the pile of dead men at the door in a growing puddle of blood—"it is fulfilled. You can't raise Jaya here. They will come after him until he's dead, forcing your people to go to war, which will be the end of us all."

It broke Ari's heart that they had to give up Jaya after just meeting him. The king and queen searched her face for options, tears spilling from their eyes.

"I will protect him," King Gurham said, his voice like gravel.

"I know. But that won't be enough. I'm sorry. I can ask Owen and Tora to take him away where no one will know him, and when he hears his calling, he'll come back, though I don't know when that will be."

"Do we have to? Do we have to send him away?" Queen Shanti pleaded, tears spilling down her face.

"No. But if you don't, it will ruin everything you have accomplished here. And he is needed to save us all when the time comes. I realize this isn't how you pictured this experience, and if there was any other option, I would suggest it."

There was such a deep note of despair and hopelessness in Ari's voice that the queen could only look at her, dumbfounded. Queen Shanti knew her son was the victor, and she'd expected to raise him as such, especially after such an early and intense labor. Usually, King Gurham fought for what was right with every fiber of his being, and he knew in the core of his soul that Ari was speaking the truth. Jaya had to be sent away for his own safety and for the safety of the Seven Kingdoms.

"We can spread the word that Jaya was stillborn, which will deter your enemies and keep the peace for now," Ari said. "Unfortunately, the best way to do it is to announce it at the banquet."

"How… how can I leave my wife's side? My son?" King Gurham roared, stepping toward Ari. She didn't take it personally.

She knew his heart and that he was acting out of character because his deepest desire was being torn away from him.

"My king," Ari said with a low curtsy of submission, "I understand how you feel, and I only share this information with you so your son can have a chance at a good life and heed his calling when the time comes. Because he will, if he lives."

The king wilted. He knew Ari was only trying to save them all and that she knew things he didn't. He had to trust her for their lives and the lives of their subjects. Seeing them together broke Ari's heart, but she understood this was bigger than all of them. Now was not the time to be selfish.

"Tora will hide him in an invisibility web until we find him a good home. You can trust Tora and Owen." Ari knew this would be a small reassurance to the new parents. "I will make arrangements and return to collect Jaya when they are ready. Please savor these precious moments with your son."

With a bow, she turned and strode out of the room, her skirts dragging on the floor behind her, soaked in birthing fluids and blood. When she left the chambers, she found a secluded hallway and then broke down. It was the hardest and most heartbreaking thing she had ever had to do, to her dearest friends no less. She slid down the wall, the stone scraping her exposed back, and rested her head on her crossed arms. Then she wailed at the injustice of it all, her body shaking uncontrollably. After a while, feeling bereft, she stood, her angelic gown stiff with gore, and went to find Owen to make the necessary arrangements.

SIX

"**W**hat is this place?" Owen asked Tora.

"The forest," Tora replied, looking at the towering trees around them. Her words created clouds of mist around her mouth, hiding her buck teeth and slight underbite.

"You know what I mean," Owen snapped. Tora could be exasperating.

They were in a less dense part of the forest and had created a clearing, stomping the snow flat, so Owen had somewhere to stand and move around. He had a series of stretches that he liked to do after long journeys in the saddle to reestablish balance to his body.

"It's a place of beautiful farming people who live clean, simple lives," Tora said as she placed wood on the fire she had built. "They are kind and hard working. If he is to be the person we need him to be, this is the perfect place for him to be raised."

"Where's the house?" Owen asked, checking the package and his gear, making sure everything was secure.

"Through the trees, you'll come to a road. Hang a left, and after a short walk you'll see the farmhouse. I'll cook this food and wait here." She fussed with the fire, setting up a spit to roast the game they'd caught on the journey. They had traveled quite far in a short time, and if they were going to return right away, they needed fuel and rest first. The sooner they returned, the better. It would look suspicious if they were gone too long. After all, they needed to keep up appearances, and Ari could only make excuses for their absence for so long. Not that they needed to explain themselves to anyone. Owen followed a deer trail through the forest. He didn't have snowshoes, so he had to forge through the snowbanks. Even though he was taller than average, it was still tough going. Once he broke through the tree line, he made his way down the road to the farmhouse. He saw a thin trail of smoke coming from the chimney and was glad the house's occupants were up. The sun was about to crest over the horizon.

As he turned down their driveway, the wind picked up, urging him toward the front door.

Leaning over the chipped basin, Ellen splashed water on her face. Her breath caught at the shock of how cold the water was. How could it be that cold and not be frozen? Grabbing the towel next to the basin, she patted her face dry. Then she looked at herself in the mirror and wondered what was wrong with her. She knew it wasn't her curly auburn hair, which now had a few silver hairs speckled throughout. Her strong legs and hips made farm work easy, and she knew if she could get pregnant, the baby would be strong and healthy. A child was the only thing she had ever wanted in life. Even as a girl she'd taken care of her dolls and helped her mother keep the house, learning how to care for a family. Like every morning, she placed her hands over her heart, bowed her head, and whispered her prayer to the Creator.

"Thank you for the abundance in my life and that of my husband. Thank you for the bounty of food and friends. Thank you for our health. If I have one wish, it's for a baby to call our own." She finished with a deep breath, pushing back tears.

"Your tea is ready," her husband, David, said when she came out of the bedroom.

"Thank you." She took her seat at the kitchen table, wrapping her hands around the cup. The heat seeped into her hands, chasing away the ache in her fingers and soothing her muscles. She was about to ask David how he had slept when there was a knock at the door. David looked at Ellen in bewilderment, his eyes questioning her. They lived on a farm, just the two of them, at least a two-hour walk from anyone else. The weak winter sun had just crested the horizon, illuminating the kitchen through the window over the sink. Ellen's first thought was that it was a neighbor needing help.

David strode to the door and lifted the safety bar. A gust of wind, saturated with ice crystals, struck his face as he opened the door, causing him to stumble back and raise his arm to shield himself from the frosty blast. When the wind settled, David lowered his arm and shook himself like a wet dog, droplets of water spraying everywhere. Looking out, he saw the biggest man he had ever seen in his life. David himself was tall, but this man was huge. He wore black leather boots up to his knees with thick, well-made tan leather pants tucked into them, a three-quarter-length leather jacket lined with fur, and a wolf mantel across his shoulders over a cloak. He had broad shoulders and a barrel chest that, upon closer inspection, looked oddly lumpy. He had a deep, focused gaze, but sincerity and trust also lived there. His fur-lined hood covered most of his hair, but his beard touched his chest. David took the full measure of the man before he spoke.

"C-can we help you?" His voice sounded as scared as he felt.

"Good morning. I apologize for the early hour, but this is a matter of great importance. May I come in?" the man asked in a warm, friendly baritone. He smiled, and faint wrinkles appeared at the corners of his eyes, putting David at ease.

"Yes, of course." David stepped aside, allowing the man to enter.

As David closed the door behind the stranger, Ellen offered him a seat beside the fire where he could warm himself.

"May I offer you a cup of tea?" Ellen asked.

"That would be delightful. I have traveled far in the cold," the stranger replied, taking the cup that was offered. His large hands made the mug look like a child's teacup. As he sipped the hot drink, he looked around the room. It was a modest house, though well cared for. The longer he sat by the fire sipping his scalding tea, the more at ease he felt. This was indeed the right place. Finally, he realized the couple was staring at him.

"What can we do for you?" David asked, his voice trailing off in the hope that the stranger would share his name.

"My name is Owen, and I come with a gift."

Before Ellen or David could ask him any more questions, Owen unbuttoned his jacket and opened the flap, revealing a baby nestled against his chest. The baby was swaddled and held against Owen's heart, to protect him from the elements. He couldn't have been more than a few days old.

Ellen sucked in air and covered her mouth. He was the most beautiful thing she had ever seen. He had black hair, softer than duck down, and his rosebud lips were searching for a nipple. As she took in the golden egg glowing around him, she wondered who would give up such a precious gift. The baby blinked its purple eyes open, focusing on Owen.

Ellen giggled. Then she started to cry. Her prayers had been answered.

"This is Prince Jaya, the First of His Name, Star Born, Prince of the Seven Kingdoms. He was born the day before last to parents who longed for him and were devastated to give him up. When he was named, he became the answer to an age-old prophecy that speaks of his death and the war of darkness that would follow should he stay with his parents. It was decided to adopt him out to a land where no one knows who he is, for his safety and that of his subjects."

David and Ellen looked from the baby to Owen, then back to the baby.

"The prophecy also says he is the one to save us from the darkness. We aren't sure what that means, but we will help him when the time comes," Owen continued. "I come to you today asking you to take Jaya and raise him as your own until the call is made. I can't tell you when that will be, but I feel he will be well taken care of here and taught the value of hard work by good people."

When Owen finished speaking, Jaya let out a shrieking wail that could have woken the dead, making Ellen laugh.

"May I hold him?" she asked.

"Of course." With deft hands, Owen reached down and pulled Jaya out of his cocoon. Owen was so big that Jaya could have easily slept in one of his hands.

When Ellen touched the boy, she let out a sob, and she knew immediately that this was her son. Sure, he hadn't grown in her body, but he was already growing in her heart. As she looked down at him, she realized his golden egg was gone, and his eyes had changed to a gray-blue color. She looked up at Owen, the question clear in her eyes.

"An undetectable spell has been placed around him, so those who may come looking for him will never know this baby and Prince Jaya are one and the same. It's not harmful, just a layer of protection. I would encourage you to rename him. Please wait until I leave, though. The less I know, the better."

Ellen looked at David, who saw the happiness in her eyes. She turned back to Owen and nodded. "We will care for him like our own until his call comes." A shiver went down her spine, sealing the bond. David felt the same way.

"Do you have any questions?" Owen asked.

Ellen shook her head as she wrapped Jaya in a blanket, holding him to her chest, swaying back and forth as she crooned to him. She looked like she was born for the role. It brought joy to Owen's heart, knowing that Jaya would be safe and well taken care of.

SEVEN

TWENTY YEARS LATER

"You asked to see me?" Apala said to the man in front of her. Well, he was sort of a man. Standing tall and proud and made of intertwined roots, he was the Witness, an ancient manifestation of the Light Beings. He had asked to be sown into Mother Earth to be cared for 45,000 years ago in human time. The knots that were his eyes sparkled with wisdom, greeting Apala as his equal.

"Yes. Thank you for coming so quickly," he replied, sweeping an arm to welcome her to the Grove. "We have a great learning experience ahead of us."

"Do you mean a problem? That's what humans call them." Apala chuckled as she met the Witness's eyes. The difference in perspectives between Light Beings and humans was sometimes entertaining.

"I suppose," he replied. "Light Taker is here."

"What? I thought it was in the vault!"

"It was. He took it, planted it a few decades ago, and ever since then, events have been set in motion."

"Planted a few decades ago?" Apala asked. "Why didn't we do anything about it then?"

"We couldn't. Prophesied one or not, he was just a baby, and he didn't have the necessary skills."

"Has he been training? Is he ready?" Apala asked, hope coloring her words.

"No and no. But he is a young adult, and it is time. He knows it; he just doesn't know what the next step is."

"Are you thinking what I'm thinking?" Apala asked.

"I guess that depends on what you're thinking," the Witness replied.

"Ari can help him on the path. She has been training and is ready for the task. I've seen the contracts, and they are important to each other. In fact, they can't go much further without one another."

"Agreed."

Apala paced back and forth, her anxiety melting away with each step as clouds of dust rose around her ankles. The Witness's eyes tracked her with a serious gaze.

"Which curse did he choose to be released?" Apala asked, unsure if she wanted to know the answer.

"The Lost Ones," he whispered, the forest around them falling silent. A heavy cloud moved in front of the sun, drenching the Grove in deep darkness, which should have been impossible for that time of day. It spoke to the threatening danger of the curse.

Apala created a ball of light in the palm of her hand. Holding it up to her pale face, it illuminated the Witness's eyes in the dark.

"You can't be serious," she said.

Light Taker was one of a pair of swords forged by knowledge and light, imbued with the ancient language of breath and movement. The problem was, Light Taker's midnight-black scabbard was etched with symbols that, if energized in the correct sequence, would release curses of varying degrees. The one the Planter had chosen was the worst and most powerful curse.

"I've never been more serious in all my time. It will be a tool of great learning and growth for many. However, if he doesn't get on the correct path soon, life will cease to exist."

"I guess Ari has her path in front of her. They both do. And she may already be heading in the right direction," Apala said, finally able to take a deep breath.

"She is," the Witness replied. "Can you find her and pass along the task?"

"Absolutely. I'm just not sure how much we should tell her."

"As little as possible. As a Path Walker, she only needs the next step. And sometimes not even that."

"True," Apala agreed.

Before the tree man could say anything else, a sunbeam cut through the darkness, and Apala disappeared.

EIGHT

A ri's hazel eyes snapped open, pulling her out of a deep, restful sleep. While she could feel a presence behind her, she wasn't scared. With her next breath, she unsheathed the knife from her boot while rolling into a crouch, ready to attack. It took her a moment to focus on the intruder's eyes, and she was entranced immediately. It was Apala, and she had come with a message. Relaxing, Ari stood, the first beams from the sunrise kissing her face. The forest was just waking from its slumber as night tipped into day.

"I bid you good day, Grandmother," Ari said, sheathing her knife.

"And to you, my child." Apala was said to be older than those who first walked. No one actually knew, perhaps because no one had asked. Her silver hair was pulled back from her face, cascading in waves down her back to her waist. She had a warm, welcoming smile with eyes that were surrounded by wrinkles. Her hands, which had caught uncounted babies, were clasped loosely in front of her.

"To what do I owe the pleasure?" Ari inquired, bringing her hands over her heart and dipping her head in respect.

"The one needs help. It is time."

"I understand." Ari lifted her chin in acknowledgement. She had been studying for most of her almost 950 years and was well aware of the prophecy that was spoken when Light Bringer and its twin, Light Taker, were forged. For those who studied prophecy, it was well known, but many misunderstood it.

"Do you know where he is?" Ari asked, hoping she would at least get a starting direction.

"Due west. I was told you will get clear messages when you need them. Keep your mind open, your body fueled, and your spirit fulfilled." Apala walked soundlessly across the needles and debris that littered the forest floor.

"Thank you, Grandmother. May I offer you a cup of tea? Surely we have enough time for that."

"Yes, my child. We haven't had a good chat in a while."

Ari stoked the fire, then set the pot above the flames. Apala sat across from her. Once the tea boiled, Ari served a cup to Apala. Just then, the sun came over the horizon behind Apala, illuminating her like an apparition. She raised her gaze from her steaming cup of tea and looked Ari in the eye, sending shivers down Ari's spine.

"Beware. This walk is not like the others. Just like him, you will be challenged seemingly beyond your abilities. Take heart, for you have been preparing, and you are ready."

It was as if Ari's soul had been laid out in front of Apala to be read like a book, making Ari feel vulnerable. She wasn't sure what she had gotten herself into, and she knew she had to continue walking this path she had started twenty years ago, or it would be the end of life. She would cross that bridge when she got to it.

Once she finished her tea, Apala took her leave, disappearing into the ether while Ari's back was turned.

Ari packed her gear and then set out, walking away from the sun. She had felt this walk was coming, and she had already been heading in the right direction. Even though she didn't know the destination, she wasn't worried, and she knew her feet would take her where she needed to go as long as she kept her intention clear.

She was a Soldier of Light, part of an elite task force called the Path Walkers. As Soldiers of Light, their duty was to bring light where there was none. The Soldiers of Light fought in wars of blood and darkness and had always managed to prevail, like the sunrise driving away the darkness of night.

Within the Soldier of Light army were different fractions and specialties. Ari had a set of skills that qualified her as a Path Walker, making it her sacred duty to help those who had trouble walking the Path of Light by sharing their burden and showing them the way. Such help could come in many different ways, from providing information, to clearing walls around the fourth house in the heart space to allow for creativity, to the basics of recovering and maintaining health. It always looked different because no two people walked the same path. Ever. She had spent hundreds of years studying for this very walk, and she was happy the time had finally arrived. She had been on the move pretty much since she became a Path Walker, either walking the earth or transcending different dimensions.

As she moved toward her quarry, she mentally organized her skills, talents, and relevant knowledge about this person she was to help. She had met him decades ago, and she was excited to see him again. Of course, back then he had just been born, so he wouldn't know they had already met, or anything about his background. It was a burden she had been carrying, and she was excited to share the truth with him when the time was right. They were moving into a new era, and he was the key.

NINE

Ari popped out of the forest and entered the bustling village of Rehom, easily blending in with the crowd. The atmosphere was light; everyone knew everyone else. It was business as usual. The butcher was shouting what was available (meat pies and sausage) from his cart, the smell of freshly baked bread wafted from the bakery up ahead, and children ran through the streets.

Keeping a low profile, Ari ducked out of the way of a horse and carriage, spinning to miss a man who almost walked into her. She flowed with the street traffic, letting the rhythm carry her.

She was looking toward the town's large center fountain when a sign with a bright red mug on it caught her attention. Shifting toward it, a bell above the door chimed when she pushed it open. It was clean and well-kept and smelled like heaven—beef stew with bacon, potatoes, and carrots. Jackpot!

Stepping into the dining room, she wound through the tables until she found a bench in the back. There she settled in, setting her pack at her feet.

She took a deep breath and realized this was exactly where she needed to be. Chuckling to herself, she said a special thank-you.

After living on the land for weeks, she was happy to have a hot meal that she didn't have to catch and cook herself, followed by a warm, soft bed. Being a Soldier of Light wasn't glamorous, but it was her calling. She had other options, but she loved walking the path, listening to the earth, and being sustained by it. It kept her mind, body, and heart pure.

"Can I get anything else for you, dear?" the server asked after Ari had finished her meal. The server was also the owner and the cook.

"No, thank you. The stew was delicious." Ari had used the crusty bread to wipe her bowl clean.

"Oh, it's nothing, dear. And it's on us. The room too. A Soldier of Light never pays here. Make sure you let us know if you need anything else. Would you like some hot water for a bath sent to your room?" She looked at Ari's dusty clothes and the pack on the floor between her feet.

"That would be amazing. Thank you." Ari sighed with satisfaction, propping her chin on the heel of her palm. The din of the other diners and the warmth of the fire beside her were lulling her to sleep.

Grabbing her pack and lifting it wearily to her shoulder, she headed toward the staircase and forced her legs to carry her up to her room at the far end of the hallway. The room was sparse but clean and cozy. She dropped her pack in the corner by a small dresser with a basin and a jug of water. She undressed and washed, reveling in the hot water. After meditating, she crawled in between the deliciously soft sheets and was asleep as soon as her head hit the pillow, but not before she had slid her knife under it, just in case.

In her dream she was soaring through the snow-capped mountains, and what she saw ahead shook her to the core of her being. Fire and destruction, death and darkness. The rolling hills were covered in ash, formerly prosperous settlements reduced to nothing but fireballs. As she passed through the thick, acrid smoke, she found herself over a sprawling encampment and was horrified by what she saw. Women were being raped, men were beating each other senseless for fun, and everyone else was drunk or on their way there.

As she flew closer to the largest tent, a stooped man with dark skin pulled the tent flap aside and stepped out. His shoulders had once been broad and muscled, but they had withered away, creating a concave shape for his chest, on which his scraggly beard rested. He strode away from the tent on legs that were slightly bowed and then stopped and looked back at her. Ari wasn't intimidated until she met his eyes. Bereft of joy and happiness, they were so black they swallowed the light, perhaps never to be seen again. They were bone-chillingly terrifying. Tearing her eyes away from his, she noticed an ancient sword in a scabbard at his hip. She recognized the symbols etched into the scabbard, and once she read them, she realized if she didn't lead the one to his destination, it would be the end of life as they knew it.

With her next breath, she was standing on the steps of a castle overlooking a city. She was dressed in her ceremonial garb, her hair pulled into a tight bun on top of her head. She realized it was a day of great celebration. Below her, a parade was winding through the crowded streets toward the castle at the top of the hill. The land surrounding the castle was green and fertile, indicating that the kingdom was prosperous and happy. The king was officially being crowned that day, and it was a change of the times for the better. Even though she couldn't see his face, she knew the man riding at the front of the parade was the one to save them all. And it was her mission to help him walk the path.

She woke up with a beam of sunlight across her face and a new understanding of what she faced. Taking a deep breath, followed by a stretch that helped her recenter after the troubling dream, she got up and got dressed. It was amazing what a clean face, a full belly, and a good night's sleep could do. She was energized with clarity and ready to continue her journey. After double-checking her gear and ensuring everything was secure, she did one more scan of the room. When she was sure she hadn't left anything behind, she shouldered her pack and bounced down the stairs to break her fast.

TEN

The inn's dining room was quiet that morning, only a few tables occupied. One of them had a man slouched over it, snoring off the previous night's liquor. Sunlight beamed through the windows, illuminating the dust motes that hung in the air. As she walked along the bar past patrons eating eggs and drinking ale, one of them slapped her on the butt. Ari stopped and spun on her right heel and left toes in a smart about-face, smiling at her assailant. Because he was sitting down, their eyes were level, and when she locked his gaze, the man couldn't look away. She took off her pack and cloak, setting them on an empty chair beside him. Her leather top rippled from her neck down her torso and down her arms and legs to her feet. In its place appeared a pearlescent white skin-tight suit that reflected the light from the window behind her. Somehow it made the light dance with joy. The effect was striking. Later, when the man was repenting to his wife, he told her he had been in the presence of an angel.

"Can I help you?" Ari asked sweetly, pinning him in his seat with her intense gaze. Probing his soul with her eyes, she saw a hurt, abandoned little boy who wanted to be loved and accepted.

The man stared into her eyes without answering, eggs falling out of his open mouth.

One of Ari's natural abilities was healing. It came to her as easily as breathing. She was able to tune into ladinya and see what was in a person's heart. She could feel their losses and upsets, their loves and joys. It had been frightening for her at first when she would see someone who was very sad, yet they would tell her they were happy. It caused confusion that made her abrupt with people who were unintentionally lying to her. This had led her to become an outcast, given that she always told the truth, even if the truth wanted to stay hidden. Later in life, she realized this was a gift, and she stopped heeding what others thought or said about her. With this attitude, she had blossomed into a no-nonsense healer whose abilities were sought by kings and queens.

Ari rested one hand above his heart and the other on his back between his shoulder blades. Focusing the ladinya in the palms of her hands, she tenderly explored his heart space. What she found there wasn't unusual, just extreme. His heart was encased in a fortress built from a lifetime of rejection, bitterness, and shame. She pulsed white light into the space, working it around the densely packed emotions, like mortar around bricks.

"You abuse your wife and children because you think telling them you love them is weak," she said. "I'm here to tell you that the opposite is true. Someone who loves life and the people around them exhibits great strength by showing it. Instead, you act out like a child having a temper tantrum. Stop!" Ari said, making the man flinch under her touch. "You deserve to receive love as much as you deserve to give it."

While her gaze was locked with his and he was listening to her words, she encased each feeling with light and love. When each emotion had been acknowledged, she thanked them for being a teacher and offering forgiveness and then shifted the light to pink. Emotion by emotion, she dismantled the fortress that had taken him a lifetime to build, and the bricks crumbled into the dust from which they had been made. When she had cleared the space around his heart, she was struck by the peace, love, and joy she felt there. He had lots to give and share; he just hadn't had access to it. When the last ounce of shame was released, a tear rolled down his cheek.

"My father used to beat me. I don't want to be like him, but I don't know how to be any different," he whispered, so softly that someone standing right next to him wouldn't have heard. Ari could feel his longing in her heart through her hand.

"It's a choice. Love is a choice. And because it is freely given, it's always the best choice you can make. Now go home and apologize to your family, and spend the rest of your life trying to make up for your sins." Her sultry voice washed over him; his baptism was complete.

He nodded in agreement. With that, the pink light died, a trace of her work still streaming from his aura. He got up and walked across the dining room and out the front door. As Ari watched him go, she felt grateful that she had been in the right place at the right time and could help get him on his path. He was walking into the unknown and had come up against an obstacle he couldn't scale on his own. He thought the obstacle was on the outside, taking his frustration out on those closest to him, but instead it was a citadel around his heart, blocking the love he so desperately craved. Ari had released a lifetime of emotions trapped around his heart, allowing the light in and out, and she had only been able to do so because he wanted to walk toward love, both giving and receiving.

Her work done, she shifted back to basic traveling garb, swung her cloak around her shoulders, and grabbed her pack. Fortunately for her, he had barely touched his food, so she grabbed his plate and found a comfortable seat where she could watch the door as she enjoyed her breakfast.

ELEVEN

Ari looked up from her breakfast when the door swung open and two young men entered, ducking to avoid bumping their heads on the crossbeam over the door. One of them was favoring his right hip, and the other was jubilant with a radiant smile. They took a table by the window on the other side of the dining area, conveniently giving Ari a perfect view of them. The smiling one nodded at the bar owner and asked for two breakfasts to be brought over.

"What do you think about that, Luke?" Ben said to his cousin, smiling as he smacked his arm.

"I've asked you not to do that. And it will never work," Luke said in a deep baritone that resonated throughout the room. He was stuffing eggs into his mouth at an alarming rate. He was almost always hungry.

"Why? I've thought of everything. I've been thinking about this all night."

His laugh drawing the attention of the few conscious people in the room, Luke looked up from his plate and into his cousin's eyes. "All night, eh? Here's the thing. I know you want me because you know I'll show up, but I can't. I haven't finished healing from the accident, and I don't want to make any promises I can't keep. You know I would be there if I could, but my hip isn't ready. I'm sorry." Luke was ashamed that he'd got into an accident and couldn't help others in his community. His leg was healing slowly, and the healer had assured him that there wasn't anything more he could do, that such things took time.

Luke held back a shiver when a tingle ran down the length of his spine. He realized someone was watching him. He swiveled in his chair to find a woman staring at him. She had curly hair that was pinned in the middle of her head from front to back with a silver streak that started just off the center of her forehead. Under perfectly curved eyebrows, her hazel eyes pierced his soul, and on her lips was a giant smile that made wrinkles appear at the corners of her eyes.

Ari knew he was the one as soon as the melodious notes of his voice collided with her energy field, making her being thrum like a plucked guitar string. She held the vibration, his vibration, in her heart, simultaneously humming her naming note, septa, the seventh note of the scale. She locked the new, unique frequency in her heart. Now she would be able to find him in any dimension, from seven down. She would walk with him, and once he reached his destination, the connection would be severed. Not many people were blessed with such a gift, and it was one of the reasons she was part of the elite force of Path Walkers.

When he finished talking with his cousin, she opened her eyes, her stare boring into the back of his head as her mind focused on a single word: "Luke." His body tensed, his head snapping toward her. Perfect!

Ari held his blue-gray eyes, which shone out from under a mop of curly black hair, as he got up from his chair and limped toward her, favoring his right leg. Ari had to crane her neck to maintain eye contact. As he drew closer, she noticed he was thin, as if he hadn't grown into his frame yet. He carried himself with an air of nobility that drew her eye and raised her expectations, and she could tell he was trying to not let his hip bother him. Pulling out the chair across from her, he sank into it.

"Who are you?" he asked.

"That's not important. What's important is, who are you?" She pointed at his nose. He was distracted by her sultry, mellifluous voice. As it washed through his being, he realized his life would never be the same, but the sensation was accompanied by a feeling of lightness as the tension around his heart, which he hadn't been aware of until that moment, eased. Luke wasn't sure what this woman wanted from him. He was just a farm boy who lived with his family. He wasn't anyone special.

"I don't understand," Luke said, his eyes full of questions.

"Here's the thing," Ari replied with a shrug, "I don't either. And that's OK because it's not for us to know right now. What I do know is you are not walking the path, and you need to be. I noticed you were limping. Did something happen?" She used her knife to pick some bacon from between her teeth.

He let out an exasperated sigh. "Yes. I was in an accident last fall, and it's taking a long time to heal. I've been told it's a process and that sometimes it takes longer than others."

"Ah, of course. May I make a suggestion?"

"Sure," he replied, although he was certain she wouldn't tell him anything he didn't already know.

"I bet it hasn't healed because you are destined for greatness, to be the light, but right now you are nowhere near the path. Good thing for you, I have been called to walk with you, and it's time to get started. We'll get our horses and be on our way."

"Wh-what?" Luke couldn't believe what he was hearing. This wasn't something he felt equipped to deal with. He just wanted to go home to his simple life.

"Horses. For our journey. The path. Greatness," Ari said, locking eyes with him.

"I'm not going on any journey with you. I don't even know you."

Ari put her knife down, leaning in to ensure she had his full attention. "So you're telling me you haven't had visions of greatness? Of leading people to a better life?" She raised her eyebrows to emphasize her question.

Luke looked away.

"How do you know about it?" Ari inquired.

"I have dreams. They've been increasing in frequency, and every time, they seem more real. Like, I'm on horseback riding through the streets at the front of a parade heading toward a castle. It's always disorienting when I wake up in my bed."

"Is this the only dream you've had?"

"No. There are two I've been having my whole life. The first one is where I'm in a field of nothingness, and when I open my eyes, I'm blinded with color. I see a kaleidoscope of rainbows, but I can't focus on one particular color or shape. Then, in a different one, there's a giant orb that's sparkling with purple and green veins running through it, but there's a black slit down the middle, like a giant void. Then the air is cold and clean, and I can hear a great drum. But it has a two-tone double beat. Like, dum-dum. Dum-dum." He banged the table with his fists to demonstrate. "It's all very comforting and steady."

Ari looked at him, awestruck. She knew they weren't dreams, and she couldn't wait until she could explain what had actually happened. Then she realized there was something in his tone that wasn't resonating with her.

"Why are you ashamed? Shame is guilt we don't talk about."

"I feel like I don't deserve greatness. I'm to stay here, farm, and raise a family. I mean, it wouldn't be the worst thing in the world. I'm just not sure it's for me." Luke's shoulders drooped as if he had accepted his fate.

"Great! Let's go! We'll start with horses."

Luke barely had enough time to process what she said before Ari stood, put on her pack, and headed for the door. When she walked by him, he finally got a good look at her outfit. She was wearing a dark green floor-length cloak with a brown leather tank top and dark leggings tucked into leather boots. He saw a knife sticking out of one of her boots, strapped to her leg. Her right forearm had a black leather armband etched with symbols he didn't recognize. Around her neck, peeking out of the bottom of her green scarf, was a gold chain with a silver charm of an anchor, a cross, and a heart that rested between her breasts. The charms were dull and looked ancient. After a moment's contemplation, he realized the charms represented faith, hope, and charity, which were the three values he stood by. On her pack was a badge that looked like a flash of white light. Beside it was another one that had a road that was half lit as if the sun were rising. Then it all came together. She was a Soldier of Light! After reaching that realization, his next thought was why she wanted him. He had grown up listening to stories about an army leading others to conquer in wars of blood and darkness. They brought light to places where there had been none and conquered that which could not be conquered. To have one target him was both unbelievable and scary.

Luke jumped up from his chair and followed her out the door as fast as his injured hip would allow. Once out in the bright sunlight, he found her walking toward the stables. That's when he made the decision that would change his life. He was going with her. He felt like he didn't have a choice. Even though he was intrigued, he was going to be cautious of this woman whom he had just met.

When he reached the stables, he stopped just outside the door, his back against the wall.

"You know how to ride?" Ari asked without turning around.

"How did you know I was here?" Luke asked, limping into the stable.

"I'll teach you," she replied as she handed him the reins of a black stallion, a sly smile on her face. "Let's get your things and then we'll be on our way. Which way is your farm?"

"It's just out of town that way," Luke replied, pointing east.

"Perfect. Mount up."

They rode hard out of the village, galloping past gawkers and leaving them in a cloud of dust. The townspeople had never seen a Soldier of Light before, let alone leading one of their own.

After rounding a bend in the road, Luke led her up a lane to his family's farm. They trotted up to Ellen, who greeted them from the small porch attached to the cozy two-bedroom home. They reined their horses to a stop, and Luke dismounted. Ari held the reins of both horses as he approached his mother.

"Luke! Where have you been? Pa has been sowing the field by himself all morning."

"Sorry, Ma. I was with Ben, and I've only come back to collect my things."

"Collect your things? What are you talking about?" she asked frantically.

"I have to go. I've been called, and she's going to help me." Luke pointed to Ari, who had dismounted and was standing next to her horse, stroking its cheek.

"Hello," Ari said. "Luke has been called, and yes, it's a surprise but not to him. This has been a long time coming." The sun was behind Ari, allowing only a silhouette of her figure to be seen and cloaking her face in shadow.

"No. No, it can't be. It's too soon." Ellen looked between the two of them, pleading for more time.

Luke took Ellen's shoulders in his large hands and looked into her eyes. "What do you mean it's too soon?" As tears streamed down her face, Luke probed her eyes for answers. Finding none, he continued. "This is something I have to do. I'm sorry. I can't stay and live the life you want for me. I've had this dream my whole life, and it's been happening more and more. Then this woman showed up this morning, and it was a confirmation of what I've been feeling for over a year. I have to go with her, and I don't know if I'll be back. I love you and Pa." He hugged her and then disappeared inside the house.

"You!" Ellen said, pointing an accusing finger at Ari.

"I know this is hard for you, and I can assure you, if there was any other option, we would pursue it. It is my sacred duty to keep people like Luke safe until they reach their destination, and I have never failed," she replied soothingly, almost with regret.

Ellen squared her shoulders and lifted her chin. "You take care of him and teach him everything he needs. He's very special and is destined for greatness."

"You need not worry. All life is forfeit if he fails."

Luke came out of the house with his pack, stopping to hug Ellen one last time. "Tell Pa I love him, and I'm sorry I couldn't say goodbye."

Ellen cupped his face with her hands and wiped a tear from Luke's cheek with her thumb. "You are our precious gift. Your father and I love you with all our hearts, and we always will. You have a great destiny, my son, and we are thankful we got this much time with you. Be safe. We love you." Ellen grudgingly accepted what was happening. They had raised Luke as their own, and she was heartbroken he had to leave, but she had always known this day would come.

Luke tied his pack to his saddle and pulled himself up. When he pivoted his horse around to face Ari, she took in a sharp breath. It wasn't Luke the farm boy on the horse; it was King Luke, ruler of the Seven Kingdoms, protector of the people. He had a gold crown with diamonds atop his brow that reflected light and created rainbows that formed a colorful halo. He was wearing a white doublet with gold embroidery, white leggings, and polished black knee-high boots. At his hip was a brilliant white scabbard with colored circles made of jewels. It was etched with symbols that Ari recognized. The scabbard was a piece of art, but it didn't compare to the ornate hilt. Wrapped around the grip was an angel with a purple gemstone embedded in its forehead. The pommel was a diamond the size of an egg that added to the halo of light around him. A white fur-lined cape was laid across his black stallion's rump. Then Ari blinked, and the vision was gone.

"We need to go," Ari said, then she turned her horse and galloped down the road.

With a final wave to his mother, Luke kicked his horse to chase her, and they rode hard for the rest of the day.

TWELVE

The Eighth Kingdom, where King Nadiri and his ancestors had been trying to rule for hundreds of years, was sandwiched between the Guru Mountains and the Virala Mountains. It was full of people who loved the land and lived off it, each with their own special magic. They understood that the Mother had given them everything, and they lived in constant gratitude for all that they had.

Their settlements dotted the land, small villages that lived in harmony and peace, trading and sharing. The only problem in the realm was King Nadiri and his ancestors trying to take what wasn't theirs. The worst part was that the king continually failed, like his ancestors, because he, like them, didn't know the land. His armies were often led into bogs, swamps, and rivers, or off cliffs. It was a waste of human life, even if his soldiers deserved to die. They were inept on the best of days. On the worst of days, they were bumbling idiots who got what they deserved.

This cycle had been going on for hundreds of generations, and all it did was improve the fighting skills of the king's enemies. Then one day it all changed. No one knew why, but suddenly King Nadiri was succeeding and gaining land and treasures, killing off the people of the land or taking them as slaves, stamping out their cultures.

King Nadiri and his army roved the land, killing everyone and everything in their path. The peaceful people would see a dust plume on the horizon and know it was all over. Their previous strategies no longer worked, and once their warriors were killed or captured, there was nothing the women and children could do but live their lives in servitude. They were stripped of their culture and their rights and beaten if they spoke their native language.

King Nadiri's great hall was adorned with tapestries of the hard-fought battles of his youth, although the tapestries had seen better days, making the room seem a bit shabby.

At the opposite end of the tall double doors was a long table on a dais with three steps leading up to it. That was where the king and his family sat. From their perch, they could preside over the court and, more importantly, the entertainment. King Nadiri sat in the middle chair, an uncomfortable seat made of hardwood shaped by the bums of his predecessors for thousands of years. To his right was Queen Isabelle, whom he had married to unite their kingdoms. While she had only given him a useless daughter, he still loved her, and he went on to rape, pillage, and grow his kingdom in her name. On his left was the smallest of the three chairs, begrudgingly added for his daughter. She was a constant source of disappointment, especially since she sought to do everything a man did. Even though he had tried to beat it out of her since he first saw her using a bow, she would not yield. The fact his wife encouraged their daughter's behavior enraged him, and he forbade his daughter, Luna, from any type of training that was meant only for men. He was too stupid to know she would do it behind his back and had been quite successful in her studies. He figured she could at least marry to grow the kingdom, and he had been looking for a possible suitor.

It was the full moon, and they were feasting. King Nadiri had demanded that seven oxen be slaughtered and served at his banquet for Queen Isabelle and his guests. He and his army had just returned from a six-month campaign, and he was celebrating his first night at home. Once, he had been battle-hardened and had a barrel chest, his arms covered with thick, ropy muscles from swinging a blade his entire life. But ever since he had found the blade at his hip, even though he had maintained his vitality, his body had deteriorated, becoming a shadow of itself. He loved war and plundering, often wearing the jewelry he found and sharing the more beautiful pieces with his queen. He had rings with large gemstones of different colors on every finger and multiple gold necklaces around his neck that would weigh down anyone else. On his head was a silver crown inlaid with rose gold and diamonds from kings past. He wore a green-and-gold doublet that matched his wife's eyes, black leggings, and knee-high black boots. He looked like a king should, except for his eyes. The irises were so dark, one couldn't tell if his pupils were dilated or not. However, the worst part was they seemed to suck in the light, absorbing it so no one else could enjoy it. The only thing darker than the king's eyes was the sword hanging from his waist in its ornate black leather scabbard.

Dancers flitted in circles in time with the music, their colorful dresses like butterflies dancing on the wind. The party was at its pinnacle when the dancers were thrown into the tables by a concussive bolt of black lightning, scattering food and drink everywhere.

In the middle of a charred circle on the floor stood a crooked man wearing a skintight silver leather suit from his chin to his toes, contoured to fit every nook and cranny of his gnarled body. Coarse silver hair stuck out in every direction from his head as if he'd been electrocuted. In contrast, the boyish grin on his gaunt face made him look approachable and helpful. However, that feeling went away when one looked into his eyes. They were completely black with jagged silver veins continually moving like untamed lightning looking for ground.

King Nadiri sprang from his seat in the middle of the table on the dais. "What is the meaning of this? Guards, seize this man!"

"You might want to rethink that," the man said with a cocky, sidelong glance at the king. Nadiri raised his hand and stopped the guards from advancing, nodding at the commander.

"Who are you, and how did you come to be in my hall?" King Nadiri demanded.

"I humbly beg your pardon, Your Majesty," the man croaked. "My name is Wizard Sloan, Zion, the Second of His Name, Light Born of the Third House." He bowed. "I have a proposition for you, and I thought it was an appropriate time," he sneered with a hint of sarcasm.

"What kind of proposition?"

"Perhaps we should speak in private," Zion suggested arrogantly.

"No!" Nadiri slammed his fist on the table, toppling a goblet and spilling wine. "I will decide when and where to speak with you. You have come to my hall uninvited, and you are not welcome. Now be gone, and don't ever come back if you like your head on your shoulders!" the king roared, spittle flying from his mouth.

King Nadiri represented such a minor threat to Zion that he strode toward the king as Nadiri uttered his threats. When the king finished his supposed intimidation tactics, Zion was close enough that a drop of spittle landed on his face. He delicately wiped it from his cheek, looking up at King Nadiri. "Tsk, tsk, tsk. I don't think you mean that," he said, addressing the king like a child. "You'll take it all back after you hear what I have to say."

With a snap of his fingers, he forced the king to lock eyes with him. Then he continued in a deathly calm voice. "I know that blade hanging at your hip," he said as he ascended the first step. "I know the depth of darkness in your heart and soul." He ascended the second step. "I know what you want." He ascended the third step. "And I know what has been denied to you."

King Nadiri gulped as Zion stood in front of him at the top of the dais. Zion saw understanding in Nadiri's eyes and knew he had gained a minion. He turned his focus to Queen Isabelle, who was sitting at the king's right.

"Good evening, Your Highness," he oozed, bowing. "Queen of the kingdom that was, or is it the kingdom that never was?"

Queen Isabelle pursed her lips, the color draining from her face as she was consumed with shame and anger.

She had grown up and ruled the Elves of Balintyne of Jest Settra. They were a culture of artisans, engineers, and warriors. Her kingdom had been prosperous and balanced until King Nadiri showed up on the doorstep, wanting it all. She knew she couldn't fight him and Light Taker, so to appease him and save her people from slavery and ruin, she had married King Nadiri, yoking their kingdoms together. After the marriage, King Nadiri spread his hate by trying to change history, and it looked like some of his lies were starting to stick. It was a daily struggle for Queen Isabelle, trying to neutralize her husband's hate, but the chore was lightened by the one bright spot in her life, her daughter, Princess Luna. Though Luna didn't have her mother's pointed ears, they had similar hair, though a different color. While Isabelle had a magenta plume that surrounded her head like the top of a dandelion, Luna's hair was light blue, a striking contrast to her gray eyes.

Zion shifted his focus to Luna, who was sitting more than an arm's length from her father's left side, as if she was just beyond his approval. He scrutinized her, searching her face. "And you, my dear … are nothing special," Zion said, returning his gaze to King Nadiri, whose face had lost its color. How did the wizard know about these things when they had never met?

With a flourish of his arms, Zion turned and addressed the room. "Now, let's finish your feast and rejoice in being home, and we can discuss my proposal tomorrow." Zion turned back to the king, plucked a grape from the tray, and popped it into his mouth. "We might as well enjoy the party!"

"Guards—" Before King Nadiri could finish his command, Zion flung his arms out from his sides, head down, palms back, and threw out a wall of light behind him that cleared everything in its path. Even though it wasn't as destructive as Zion would have liked, it still got his point across.

Zion looked up, locking eyes with King Nadiri. "Like I said, we might as well join the party and discuss my proposal tomorrow, after I have enjoyed your hospitality." Zion sneered, glaring with eyes that dealt death.

Nadiri stole a sidelong glance at Queen Isabelle, who nodded ever so slightly.

"Very well," he replied. "Join us for our feast, and we shall discuss this tomorrow—after I put a son in my wife's belly!" He hollered the last part, raising his mug and sloshing beer about. A chorus of cries answered his proclamation. With a nod from the queen, the band started playing again, and the jugglers came forward. A spot at the head table was cleared for the wizard.

THIRTEEN

After a satisfying night with a few of the court's women, Zion was given an audience with the king. They met in King Nadiri's favorite room in the high tower that looked across his newly acquired land and the Guru Mountain Range in the distance. If he didn't like what one of his advisors said, he would throw them out the window, their bodies exploding on the rocks below.

King Nadiri pulled his attention away from the slave filling his goblet and looked at Zion. "Why did you come to my court? And how?" He had never seen such sorcery before.

"You wouldn't understand the how, and I already told you the why," Zion replied pompously.

"I was asking for the details," King Nadiri said, his jaw clenching in annoyance.

"Oh. Well, then you should have said that. Clear communication is the key if we are to work together. You would do well to remember that." Zion locked eyes with the king, ignoring his request. This surprised King Nadiri, as the wizard was the only one to meet his gaze since he had acquired Light Taker. His wife said it was because to meet his eye was to look into the very depths of the underworld. They sucked the light from the room, spreading darkness.

"Hmph."

Zion stood up and started pacing, Nadiri's inky black eyes following him like a hawk. The slave shuffled to the corner of the room to give Zion lots of space to move around the huge table, which seated twelve.

"Your actions on the battlefield have come to my attention, and I have developed a plan to take over the continent," Zion said, his back to the king as he looked out the window.

"Take over the continent? Including the Seven Kingdoms? It can't be done," King Nadiri said with disbelief, waving his goblet around and sloshing wine onto the table. A slave appeared with a cloth to mop up the mess.

It annoyed King Nadiri when the slaves got too close to him, but once his wife had explained that they needed to get close to serve, it didn't bother him as much. In fact, he didn't care who served him, as long as he got served. At least this slave was unassuming, wearing tan pants and a brown tunic over a long-sleeved blouse. A wide belt kept his tunic in place. The slave was clean with short dark hair, an oddly bulbous nose, and crooked teeth. For a moment, the king considered talking to his wife about only letting attractive people serve him, but the thought fled his mind when Zion turned around and sneered at him.

"Just because you don't think it can be done doesn't make it impossible."

"What's in it for me?" King Nadiri asked, draining his cup and then motioning to the slave for a refill. Grabbing the pitcher of wine, the slave scurried over, avoiding Zion, then filled the cup and retreated to the safety of the corner.

"You would be the head of the people, those who were left." He chuckled to himself. "And you could do with them whatever you pleased."

"And what do you want?" Nadiri asked, drumming his fingers on the arm of his chair.

"That's no one's business but mine. I can guarantee we don't want the same thing, and when we're done, I'll have what's mine."

He stopped pacing and looked out the window, his oddly crooked body making a creepy misshapen shadow on the wall behind him.

King Nadiri drummed his fingers on the arm of his chair as he pondered the thought of ruling the entire continent. He had been trying to rule it his whole life and had been thwarted every time. He had been buying time and building his army, and this could be his opportunity to finish what he had started.

"How do I know I can trust you?"

"You don't," Zion said, turning to look at the king.

"What's the plan?" Nadiri asked after a moment of contemplation.

"Since the sword on your hip has come into play, its opposite must have too. Pray tell, how did you acquire that unique and ancient weapon?"

King Nadiri had a frightened look in his eyes, but it was so fleeting, Zion wondered if he had actually seen it.

"About two decades ago, we were on the losing side of a campaign, and a bad storm drove those of us who were left to seek shelter in a cave. I went in deeper to explore, and I found the sword lying against a rock. When I pulled it from its scabbard, a black wave and a screeching sound erupted from the blade. Actually, every time I pull it free of its scabbard, it makes the same screeching sound. The hilt fit so well in my hand that I couldn't help but take it. I have been fighting with it ever since, mastering it through my war efforts."

Zion frowned. "It didn't call you? You found it?"

"Correct." King Nadiri raised his goblet in a mock salute.

"Interesting. So, who would have found it, and why didn't they keep it?" Zion mumbled to himself. "I could link it to me or link Light Bringer to him..."

"It's my sword," Nadiri said, sounding like a sniveling child who had been sent to bed without dessert. "I've used it in battle to kill hundreds of people."

"So you don't know its significance?" Zion asked, resuming his pacing.

"It doesn't matter. It's mine, and I'll do what I want with it."

"I understand," Zion said, wanting to placate the king. "But what if I told you it's an ancient blade of unimaginable power that released a curse when you pulled it from the scabbard and that I can use its twin to raise an army that can't be killed?"

King Nadiri stared at Zion, slack-jawed. "Does this blade have a name? And what kind of curse?" This news seemed too good to be true.

"It's name is Light Taker, and it's curse doesn't allow the souls of recently killed people from leaving their corpses to find the light of everlasting life, so they are ripe for the picking."

King Nadiri placed his hand on the pommel. "Light Taker?" As the words fell from his mouth, the sword hummed under his hand with the need to be released. "How are they 'ripe for the picking?'" he asked, looking for holes in the plan.

"That's for me to worry about. You've done the hardest part already, and you just need to keep doing what you're doing." Zion was only sharing what was absolutely necessary.

"I don't believe you," Nadiri replied.

"Even after what you saw me do last night?"

Nadiri didn't know what to think. His ancestors had been trying to expand their kingdom for generations, with little to show for it. Could this be the opportunity he'd been waiting for?

"Let's say I decide to team up with you. What's the next step?"

Their attention was pulled from their conversation when the slave dropped the pitcher of wine, smashing it on the floor and splattering wine over his feet. Thankfully, the pitcher had been almost empty, so the mess was manageable.

"Sorry, m'lord. Excuse me, m'lord," the slave gruffly said, dropping to his knees and collecting the pieces of the shattered pitcher, then mopping up the mess.

"Does that mean you're in?" Zion asked, returning his attention to the king. "We'll do a Handshake of Certainty and then I'll tell you everything you want to know."

"What's a Handshake of Certainty?"

"It's a handshake that has a spell that, if broken, will result in the betrayer's death and a curse of ill health laid on his or her lineage."

Zion approached the king, indicating he should rise from his chair. Once standing, it took a moment for King Nadiri to regain his balance. Maybe he had had too much to drink. Who was he kidding? There was no such thing!

Standing eye to eye, the stooped battle-hardened king and the crooked wizard grasped opposite forearms, crossing one over the other.

"Repeat after me," Zion croaked, probing the king's soul with his eyes. "I, King Nadiri, henceforth will not take action against Wizard Sloan, Zion, the Second of His Name, Light Born of the Third House. If I do so, I forfeit my life, leaving those behind me in line unable to produce a healthy heir." King Nadiri repeated the wizard's words. When he finished, white light and inky darkness intermingled and swirled around their linked arms, creating a figure eight. It snapped closed around their wrists like handcuffs, surprising Nadiri, who tried to pull his arms back. It was so tight it left a ring of bruises around their wrists. Just as he was about to call the guards, the cuffs blew apart, and the energy dissipated throughout the room, stirring up dust. The slave in the corner covered his mouth and coughed in response.

"It is done," Zion said, peering down his nose at the king.

"If you say so," Nadiri replied, massaging his wrists. "Now, what's the next step in your grand plan?"

FOURTEEN

King Nadiri and Zion sat across from each other laying out their plans, the slave ever vigilant in the corner. Their meeting was cut short by Zion when King Nadiri started slurring his words. Zion wasn't angry; in fact, he was glad the king was showing his true colors. Zion had been threading personal questions throughout the conversation, learning about the king's fears and what made him tick. It was almost too easy. He stood up and strode to the door.

"You continue enjoying yourself, and I'll let you know when I need you," Zion said over his shoulder. The words "I need you" echoed in the stairway, which the slave found interesting.

The slave turned his attention from the doorway to the king, who was trying to find his balance after standing up. Mumbling in a drunken stupor, he stumbled toward the doorway, reaching out to brace himself on the doorframe. The slave was embarrassed for the king, but he dared not help.

In truth, the slave was not actually a slave. The slightly stooped, dark-haired, bulbous-nosed, crooked-toothed young man was actually King Nadiri's daughter, Princess Luna. She was hard working and had special gifts that she kept secret. Her mother had ensured she could train in anything she could get her hands on ever since she could walk. This included, but was not limited to, bow and arrow, sword, javelin, ax, hand-to-hand combat, scouting, map reading, history, etiquette, how to lose a war (from her father's records), and her personal favorite, being incognito. What better place to up the ante in an exercise in stealth and deception than the meeting with the wizard and her father?

She counted to one hundred after her father left, then collected the pieces of the broken pitcher and the goblet onto a tray. Balancing it on her shoulder, she made her way down the tight spiral staircase.

The trick to a good cover was the story and one's commitment to it. She'd served as a slave, so she'd clean as a slave. Also, it was surprisingly easy to walk through the castle without being confronted when one looked busy.

As she entered the kitchen, she was hit with delicious, mouthwatering smells. Say what one would about her father, he knew good food. Leaving the goblet with the dishwasher, she threw the broken pieces in the recycling bin and then added her tray to the top of the stack. Walking toward the door leading to the yard, she pulled off the fake nose and dropped it into her wig, along with the fake teeth. She took off her belt and pulled the tunic over her head in one motion, her hair springing back into place. She bundled the costume into a ball and handed it to her best friend, Daphne, who entered the kitchen as Luna was leaving. The exchange happened so smoothly that Luna was able to throw the black cloak Daphne gave her around her shoulders and secure it around her neck just as she reached the door. Without missing a step, she shifted from a stooped manservant to Princess Luna.

She marched through the yard like she had somewhere to go, which she did. As she turned toward the stable, Edward called from the training yard, "Luna! Why don't you come over and show us how it's done?" He wasn't teasing her. He and the other trainees genuinely wanted to learn from her. She was always up for teaching, but today she had something else to do.

"Sorry, boys. You'll have to get along without me today. I have somewhere to be," she replied saucily as she strutted into the barn.

Luna knew her horse, Star, would have heard her voice and would be excited. When Luna walked around the corner, sure enough, Star had her head out of her stall, waiting. As Luna got within touching distance, Star started prancing back and forth across her stall. Luna laughed at how ridiculous Star looked. Tiptoeing to the corner, Star picked up a branch that she had saved from their last outing. Holding it in her mouth, she lifted it over the stable door and dropped it at Luna's feet. She looked expectantly at Luna and the stick, hoping for a game of fetch. The performance reminded Luna of a rambunctious puppy.

"We don't have time for that today," Luna explained as she opened the door and threw the branch back into the corner. Star sobered immediately. Standing straight and tall, her chest thrust out, she was ready for work.

Luna harnessed her, leading her to the saddling area. She lovingly brushed Star's glossy gold coat, making it as shiny as a polished coin. She threw a blanket on Star's back, followed by a white saddle trimmed in pearls. Luna had made it herself, ensuring the blue shimmer matched her hair perfectly. If Star had been any taller, Luna would have had to stand on a stool to reach over her back.

When Star was saddled up, she shook from her head to her rump, tossing her silky mane and tail. Once settled, she walked to Luna, who was waiting patiently by the door. They stepped out of the barn together into the yard, stopping in a ray of sunshine. Putting her foot in the stirrup, Luna got comfortable in the saddle. She looked around the yard and realized everyone was looking at them in awe. Luna didn't know what they were looking at, so she dismissed any notion of what they actually saw, which was a glittering golden horse saddled in a gleaming white saddle with a strong, powerful woman on her back. The pair glowed with ethereal light that made them seem like messengers sent by God himself.

Dismissing the looks, Luna turned Star toward the drawbridge and clicked her tongue. Star took off at a haughty trot, knowing the light dancing off her coat made her look magnificent.

FIFTEEN

Luna and Star came to a clearing deep in Jest Settra, the forest of her mother's people, the Elves of Balintyne. Her mother had saved the forest by marrying her father, only one of her motivations. Luna went there often to meditate, Ask, Listen, and Think. She had a special gift that she had kept a secret her whole life. Luna was "the Answer." That's what she called herself anyway. She would ask a question and know the Answer.

What Luna didn't understand was that when she asked a question with the intention of gaining Truth, she was creating space for a matching frequency, also known as the Answer. Simply put, by creating the frequency of the question, she created the frequency of the Answer. She could feel it and then interpret it.

She had never blocked it, only nurtured and honed it. She didn't abuse her gift because she felt that some questions shouldn't be answered, and other questions weren't hers to ask. Also, what was the fun in knowing everything?

She knew if her father found out about her gift, he would imprison her and torture her to ask questions. Obviously, she couldn't allow him access to her power, so as a deterrent, she had trained and gained knowledge, tricking him. The only one who knew was Star, and Luna had sworn her to secrecy.

She secured Star's reins so she could wander and not get caught on a branch. Taking a moment to stroke Star's soft coat, she thanked her for the ride and the friendship. Star responded by wrapping one of her legs around Luna's waist. With a final pat, Star turned into the forest, nose to the ground, sniffing like a hound dog, securing the perimeter. Every now and then, Star would find an irresistible clump of grass, ripping it from the ground for a tasty morsel. Luna shook her head at how awesome her friend was, then turned toward her den.

She had stumbled across the hollow tree one day when out exploring. The bottom of the ancient tree's trunk had been burned out, creating a lovely little space to sit and ponder.

Bending over, Luna walked inside and covered the doorway with branches, so she wouldn't be immediately visible to passersby. It was unlikely anyone would wander by, but she couldn't be too safe.

Sitting in front of the altar on the cedar boughs she had collected, she made an offering of an acorn, setting an intention of wisdom. She had a moon rock in the middle surrounded with unique rocks that she had found on her travels. One had golden specks in it, one was green and translucent, and another was smooth and black. Another was in the shape of a heart. Star had found that one. Luna had added branches that she changed out with the seasons along with different types of dirt and sand.

Settling down, she focused on the illuminated altar before her. When her eyelids became too heavy, she closed them, then inhaled the forest air, paying attention to her breath. In and out, down and up, down and up. She let the cool, damp waves cleanse her worries as the air penetrated her body. It energized her muscles and brain, creating space. When she was full, she bowed her head to her heart, dropping her ego and logic, and stepping into love, trust, and creativity. Fully relaxing her mind, she opened herself to the ether, now in a trance.

"What is Light Taker?"

"*The sword to end life, as it is known.*"

That was bad.

"How?"

"*Being the tool to release the curse of the lost ones.*"

"Who are the lost ones?"

"*Souls who are bound to the earth, unable to find peace everlasting.*"

"Where are they?"

"*In the earth.*"

Duh. She could have sworn she heard the smallest hint of sarcasm in the reply.

"How are they going to end life?"

"*They will be raised as an indestructible army, destroying whatever their master deems.*"

This was the army Zion was talking about. That was one mystery solved.

"What method will they use to end life?" Luna asked after working to frame the question correctly, so she would receive the answer she was looking for.

"*The lost ones will devour life, creating the void.*"

A cold feeling of dread swept through Luna, making her think she should have worn her bearskin jacket. It felt as if the life had been sucked out of her. Did she still exist? How could she exist in a place that didn't exist in a time that did exist? Nowhere was everywhere, and everywhere was nowhere.

Luna slammed her psyche closed, breaking through the vision and leaning forward on her hands, her tranquility shattered. Breathing hard, with sweat dripping from her brow, she tried to fathom what she had just experienced and realized that if she thought about it too hard, she would go mad. She couldn't let that happen lest someone learn about her gift and take her captive to abuse it.

Star neighed and stamped her hoof. Luna could hear the anxiety in her movements.

"It's OK. I'm almost done."

Star snorted in acknowledgement.

Finding her breath, Luna steadied herself and once more bowed her head to her heart.

"What is my father's role in this?"

"*To release the curse and create the army of the lost ones.*"

So, he had already done half of what was required.

The pieces were falling into place. She remembered the day her father came home with jewels and slaves, a new sword at his hip, one she had never seen before. She didn't think much of it, assuming it was part of his plunder, like everything else. She never would have guessed it had released a curse. But it explained how her father had suddenly started to prevail after generations of failure.

"How do I stop it?"

"*You don't,*" the voice boomed in her mind.

"Is there anything I can do?"

"*Be you.*"

That wasn't helpful. Who else would she be?

"Is there anything I can *do* to help?" She couldn't just sit by and watch this happen. She had to do something!

"*Release the light.*"

Not helpful. Did that mean lighting a fire? Holding a lantern?

"Is there anything else I can do?"

"*No.*"

OK. So that was that.

She was careful not to abuse her gift. She had realized at a young age that carrying too many answers wore her spirit down, and if she wanted to be as clear as possible, she needed to be smart and efficient when using her gift.

She felt like she had received all the information she could handle for one day. Stumbling from her den, she pulled herself into Star's saddle, but the weight of the answers proved to be too much. She slumped over Star's neck and awakened in her bed two days later.

SIXTEEN

When the sun touched the western horizon, Ari led Luke to a campsite.

"This is one of the places where I camped on my way to find you. It will be suitable for tonight. I'll take care of the horses, and you can start a fire."

They worked in relative silence. Ari hummed as she cleaned and watered the horses and then left them on long leads, so they could graze. She occasionally mumbled and giggled under her breath as if answering a question. Was she talking to the horses? Luke still wasn't sure about Ari, but he knew he had to trust her.

After she had put all the ingredients in the pot for stew, she stood back and closed her eyes. Taking a deep breath, her clothes changed. Starting just under her chin, a lightweight forest camouflage material appeared and flowed down her body. Her leather shirt and dark pants disappeared. In their place was an elegant, shimmering bodysuit. Luke squinted, trying to see the details in the firelight. When he leaned in, he noticed her bodysuit looked bumpy and shiny. Then he realized it was covered in millions of tiny scales.

Ari opened her eyes and saw him watching her. He leaned back on his arms, shaking his head in disbelief and muttering to himself. "It can't be possible. Then again, what is possible?" The corners of Ari's mouth quirked up at that last comment.

She looked down at him, meeting his gaze. "Your eyes will always deceive you." She flicked her wrist, snapped her fingers, and the suit changed again. Her hair was pulled into a tight bun on top of her head, the silver streak highlighting the bun's spiral twist. Her bodysuit had shifted to a magnificent formal gown. The high-neck, long-sleeve, dropped-waist top was covered in diamonds, making the firelight dance with joy. Before Luke was blinded, he shifted his gaze to her white bell skirt, which had lengthwise ruffles that were trimmed in gold. The image would be burned into Luke's mind for the rest of his life as one of the most beautiful things he had ever seen.

With another flick and a snap, the gown disappeared. In its wake was a wide-brimmed hat slanted over one eye, which was covered in an eye patch. The back of the hat touched her tall collar, which wrapped around her neck and framed her face. The collar belonged to a long jacket that had a wide belt wrapped around her hourglass waist secured by a large gold buckle. On her feet were low-heeled boots that reached past her knees. Her jacket was rippling blues and greens on a background of black with an angry ocean storm. The longer Luke looked at it, the dizzier and more nauseous he felt. On her hip hung a sword with an ornate hilt. It was shocking and fierce and made Luke wonder where such an outfit would be appropriate.

Then the first version of her bodysuit reappeared.

Luke followed her every move as she sat and ladled out the stew, then handed him a steaming bowl. "It was a gift from a dear friend," she said as if that explained where she had gotten a shimmering bodysuit, whose color and design she could change with a snap of her fingers. "That's a story for another time."

He took the bowl after she prodded his attention back to the task at hand. Blowing on his stew between mutterings, he finally managed to get it all down.

Afterwards, when they were sipping tea, Luke decided it was time to ask his questions. The only problem was, which one to ask first?

"Who are you?"

"I already told you, it doesn't matter," Ari replied over the crackling of the fire. The flames reflected off her suit, illuminating her face with a dancing light.

"Yes it does. If I'm to trust you and follow you, I want to know more about you."

"That's fair. But you aren't following me; you're walking with me. Technically, I'm walking with you."

"What's the difference?" he asked, his head tilted in curiosity.

"When you follow someone, you aren't in the lead or in charge. You're not making your own decisions or living your life the way you want. When you walk with someone, you are equals working together toward the same goal. That's what we're doing. You could get to where you're going; I know this. However, with me and my gifts, the path will be quicker and easier."

Luke looked sideways at Ari. He knew exactly what she was talking about. He had been feeling for a long time that farm life wasn't for him, but he didn't know what else to do or where else to go. And now he had answers.

"So, who are you?" he asked again.

Ari lowered her bowl and looked at Luke as she contemplated her reply. The less he knew about her the better it was for both of them.

"My name is Ari, and I have spent almost my entire life training for this very walk. I have a specific set of gifts that have been nurtured and honed through trials and tribulations that have made me part of the elite force of Path Walkers as a Soldier of Light. Does that answer your question?"

Luke was dumbfounded. He had never in a million years thought that a Soldier of Light, let alone a Path Walker, would ever find him, and now he was having tea with one. He knew only a few were called to be Path Walkers, and not much was known about them. That was probably the way they wanted it.

"You can close your mouth."

Luke snapped his mouth shut, shaking his head as he tried to reboot his brain. He hadn't realized his jaw was hanging open. He decided to test her.

"You mentioned special gifts. What can you do?"

Ari chuckled. "That's for me to know and you to find out. It's safer for both of us if you don't know."

"Just one?"

After a moment of contemplation, she nodded. "OK. Sit comfortably, close your eyes, and take a few deep breaths." She stood up and walked around the fire, then sat beside him.

Luke sat cross-legged, his hip throbbing from riding hard, causing pins and needles to shoot down his leg and making it cramp. When he shifted to relieve the pain, fire shot up his back and into his head, coursing through the right side of his body. He only realized he was holding his breath when Ari reminded him to release the air and take a deep breath. He was in so much pain, she had to walk him through it.

When he had relaxed enough to breathe deeply on his own, Ari put one hand on his hip and the other on his forehead. Probing the space in his hip, she noticed he had a big block that looked like a dense black ball of ladinya. She hummed while bringing green translucent light into the blockage. After a few deep breaths, the green light penetrated the dark ball and expanded it from the inside, causing the molecules of dark energy to oscillate. When the darkness was about to explode, Ari shifted the green light to white, pulled it into her body, and blew it out in a shock wave that lifted the hair away from Luke's face. When she stepped back, Luke opened his eyes and took a deep breath. He laid down with his hands on his belly and his eyes closed.

"Are you OK? It's normal to need to lie down after this type of work." Her voice mixed with the humming sensation that he felt in his entire being.

"I'm good," he slurred, giving her a thumbs-up.

After a few minutes, he rolled onto his side and sat up, cross-legged. He noticed there was no pain, discomfort, or shooting pins and needles down his leg or up his back. Closing his eyes, he took several deep breaths, feeling them throughout his body. Then he stood, holding his arms out to his sides to maintain balance. When he was steady, he jumped and walked around.

"How does it feel?" Ari asked.

"Incredible! How did you do that? I had the accident last fall and was told I'd probably never be back to normal. Now, no pain, no discomfort, and I can breathe easier." Astonished, he rotated his hips in circles, taking deep breaths and feeling his lungs expand to their maximum. "I haven't been able to do that for six months. Unbelievable."

"Second lesson. The essence, that of which everything is made, is called ladinya. It is meant to move, sometimes so slowly it doesn't look like it's moving at all and sometimes so fast we can't consciously believe. Sometimes it lumps together and compresses enough to create the building blocks of everything physical." She interlocked her fists to demonstrate her point.

"What do you mean 'compresses enough'?" Luke asked as he paced around the campsite to integrate the work they had done.

"It means there are different levels, frequencies, and dimensions. For example, there are sounds humans can't hear, but animals can. I can train you to tune into your Senses and use them to your advantage to gather information from your environment. You can train your eyes to see colors around people, your ears to hear Truth, and your field to gather information."

She raised her eyebrows as if to ask Luke if he understood. Luke nodded, his eyes wide in awe.

"Humans can manipulate ladinya adhascetana, meaning they don't know they are doing it, or cetana, with intention, which I'm going to teach you." She held her hand up to discourage Luke from asking questions. He didn't have all the pertinent information, and she would be answering his questions anyway.

"When ladinya doesn't flow properly, blocks are created. If not released, blocks can cause dis-ease or, in your case, lack of healing from trauma. In your hip, you had a condensed ball of ladinya that was so dense you couldn't remove it yourself because it was attached to trauma that you didn't directly experience. The ladinya wasn't able to flow, so healing couldn't occur."

"How did you move it?" Luke asked.

"I have a special ability, honed through a lifetime of practice, to tune in to the frequency and then change it and move it. In your case, I increased the frequency by saturating the blockage with love until the frequencies matched. Then it dissipated, allowing the ladinya to disperse and flow naturally through the area, also known as healing."

Luke looked at her like she had horns growing out of her head. She was used to it. "How did it get stuck in the first place?"

Ari's eyes lit up. "That's an excellent question. As human beings, we chose to come to the earthly plane, a specific dimension, to experience what being a human is all about, which is feeling and experiencing emotions. 'Emo' means energy, and 'motion' means moving, hence, energy in motion. Emotions are a specific set of frequencies, and if they aren't processed properly, they get stuck. Sometimes two of them stick together, creating their own unique frequency. That's tricky to remove, but it can still be done."

"Does everyone have these blocks?"

"To some degree, yes. We don't always have the space we need to process all the ladinya in the moment. Sometimes it's too much, sometimes it's too intense, sometimes it's not even yours, and sometimes it's all three." She paused to let the information sink in. She could feel Luke processing everything, and she didn't want to overwhelm him.

"How do you get rid of it? Is it stuck forever?"

"There are a few ways. Being thankful and grateful can help dislodge some of it. You can also ask a trained professional, like me, to help, and you can use tools like the Ballet of Breath, which uses your breath to force the blocks to release. And before you ask about the Ballet of Breath, that's a different conversation for another day. Any other questions?"

"Yes. You said sometimes the block isn't ours. How can we carry around things that don't belong to us?"

"Ladinya is shared when you interact with others, whether humans, animals, or plants. Sometimes we share emotions with the people we experience them with, and we take them on. The more common way of getting others' emotions is through our ancestors. When a child is born, they carry all the information from every single person in their heritage. They take on trauma, and sometimes it's quite deep for a prolonged time over multiple generations. When layered on with current trauma, it can cause negative behavior that breeds hate because people are so bogged down trying to maintain the façade of safety. If the ladinya hasn't been cleansed or cleared, a person could be walking around weighed down with hundreds of generations of junk—that's a technical term, by the way." She chuckled to herself as if understanding an inside joke. "And that junk helps mold them into the person they are. Unfortunately, most of the inherited stuff isn't good and can unknowingly make someone a bad person, almost through no fault of their own. Those are the saddest cases.

"We can manipulate ladinya not only through our emotions but also through our thoughts. When you have a thought in your mind, you are sending a vibration, faster than you could possibly imagine, out into the ether, which brings the same vibration back to you. The ether is like an invisible goo that connects all of us."

"Is that like when you think of someone you haven't talked to in a while and then you bump into them the next day?"

"Yes! That's correct." She was pleased with how quickly he'd understood.

Luke's mind raced with the implications. As his understanding deepened, he became overwhelmed, his breath quickening. He was starting to understand what was required of him, and he knew if he didn't have Ari's help, they would all be doomed.

"Luke, breathe," she said. "I'm here to help, and if we need more help, all we have to do is ask. You are not alone."

Ari's voice helped fan the stress away. He felt comforted and realized that whoever Ari was, he would be with her until the end.

SEVENTEEN

A ri awoke in the darkest part of the night, her breath clouding her face. She moved to a spot in their camp where she could keep an eye on Luke, who was still asleep, curled in his cloak next to the dying fire. Shifting her bodysuit to its original form and color, she checked Luke again. When she was certain he was safe, she started her ritual.

Sitting on the ground, she placed her hands over her heart and closed her eyes, then set her intention for the day. This was what she would try to embody as she walked through the world. That day she chose to step into trust, certain that everything would be well and that they were on the right path.

She tipped forward, placing her hands in the dirt and unfolding her legs until she was on all fours. Splaying her hands, pointer fingers forward, she raised her hips to the sky, creating a triangle with her body. Putting the weight of her upper body onto the bottom knuckles of her pointer fingers, she used them as energetic anchors and launching points. Feeling the pulsing earth energy, she tapped into it, using her breath to pull it in through her hands. It flowed up her arms, through her shoulders, and up her back, popping vertebrae as it climbed. Moving through her upper back and chest, she folded it back on itself around her heart, using it to cleanse and caress, magnifying the gratitude and thankfulness she felt there.

When she finished inhaling, the energy pooled in the highest point on her body, her pelvis. The energy rode the tide of her exhalation down her thighs, shins, calves, and out the four corners of her feet. The circle was complete, and she gave herself to it, allowing the earth to show her where her body was blocked. Lifting one heel, then the other, she rocked her hips back and forth, bending the opposite knee. Stopping for an extra breath in stillness, she Listened. When she didn't receive any direct messages, she continued to move her body, allowing the energy to shift her posture and filling a need she craved. She inhaled, nurturing herself with the low frequency of beautiful Mother Earth. It fanned her core with oxygen and inspiration, preparing her for the day.

When at last she was satiated, she lay still, allowing complete integration and harmony with her body, mind, and spirit. When she was nudged aware by completion, she wiggled her toes, gently restoring control. Working her way up her body, she rolled onto her right side, using her arm as a pillow. She pushed herself up, bringing her head up last, then sat with her hands clasped over her heart. Her body was humming like a tuning fork, open to communication with the universe. Her eyes still closed, she bowed her head, the rising sun kissing her face.

She opened her eyes and looked to her left, meeting Luke's awestruck gaze. "That was unlike anything I've ever seen," he said. "Graceful, magical, strong. What was that?"

"That is an ancient language and practice called the Ballet of Breath. Created by the light beings from the Otherside as a tool to bring ladinya into the body, allowing for alignment and movement." After dusting off her feet, she pulled her boots on. "By shifting your body into different shapes or poses, you can create different frequencies, thereby—

"Creating different emotions," Luke said.

She laughed. "Yes! That's exactly right. Not only can emotions be created, so can qualities, and all of them are represented in the Ballet of Breath."

She stood and started saddling her horse, nodding at Luke to do the same.

"Wow," he said, joining her. "Does everyone know about this? I feel like it could be disastrous."

"It would be, so no, not everyone knows. Soldiers of Light do. In fact, it's one reason why we can be Soldiers of Light. It's a large part of our training, so we can move through the houses—which is a different conversation for another day."

"Can anyone learn it?"

"I feel the question you're actually asking is, can *you* learn it. The answer is yes. In fact, it's one of the things you need to know. I'm glad you're such a willing student."

"How long have you been studying?" he asked over his horse's back.

"Pretty much my whole life. I find it fairly intuitive, and I understand it as well as the person who brought it here."

"The person who brought it here? What do you mean by that?" He double checked the straps on his saddle bags. Before Ari could answer, the hair was brushed off Luke's forehead by the draft of the biggest raven he had ever seen. It perched on a tree branch above his head and cawed, getting their attention.

"What is it?" Ari stopped what she was doing to look at the bird.

"Caw, caw!" was all Luke heard, but Ari heard something different: "A score of men are heading this way, looking for him."

"How long?"

The raven cawed in response.

"We need to go *now*," Ari exclaimed, mounting her horse. She took off at a gallop, Luke close behind.

The horse's consistent cadence allowed her to meditate and tune in to who or what was after them. She concluded it had to be the orders of the man with the light-devouring eyes from her dream.

After riding hard for several hours, she brought her lathered horse to a halt and leaped out of her saddle.

"Take the horses and ride into the forest that way," she said. "Keep going, and don't stop. I'll find you. Now go!" She threw the reins of her horse at Luke.

"But what if you don't find me? Where are you going? What's going on?" Luke asked, his voice frantic.

"I'll explain everything later. You need to go now!" She slapped his horse's rump, and it took off at a gallop. Ari chuckled at the dumbfounded look on Luke's face as their horses crashed through the forest, carrying him away from the threat.

Ari stood in the middle of the road, her eyes closed and her arms at her sides. She could feel the thunder of the enemy horses' hooves through her boots as they searched for their quarry. When she realized what direction they were coming from, she turned that way to gather information. Bowing her head, she loosened her Senses, sending out waves of ladinya that gave her feedback about her environment. There were twenty-five men and horses. They had lances, swords, and knives. She didn't sense any crossbows, and she thanked the Creator for that. Because she was alone, this was vital information, and she used it to plan her attack, eliminating the threat as quickly as possible. She and Luke didn't have time to be running off course.

As the men approached and saw her standing in the middle of the road, they slowed their horses.

"Where is he?" a blond man demanded.

"Where is who?" Ari inquired nonchalantly, tossing her cape over one shoulder and then checking her nails for dirt.

"The one. We know you are traveling with him. Now where is he?"

"I don't know who you're asking about," she replied, feigning innocence, a mild threat laced through her words.

"We know he's with you. Hand him over!" the man shouted, sending crows flying from their perches in surprise.

"Tell you what, why don't you take your men and run back to whoever told you I'm supposedly helping some kid before you hurt yourselves?" Ari said, giving the blond man an opportunity to save his life and the lives of his men. Rather than take her up on her suggestion, the man's face turned red in frustration. "You don't have to do this," Ari continued. "You can turn around and live a happy life. If you don't, I promise these will be your last moments." Her deadly tone made the men freeze where they were. She couldn't take the chance of them getting to Luke. Once they decided to hurt her friends or innocents, the soldiers' lives had become forfeit.

"Last chance!" the man shouted. "Give us the boy!" He dismounted from his horse and drew his sword.

As the man harassed her with threats, the rest of his party dismounted and surrounded her. She knew they wouldn't hesitate to kill her to get to Luke. Fortunately, Luke was nowhere to be found.

As they unsheathed their weapons, she took another deep breath, then shook her head with regret. These men were clear in their intention, and from that space, Ari chose to show them the path to the afterlife because of the choices they had made. This was not a decision she made lightly. She hated this part.

Taking a centering breath, she imagined her bodysuit as midnight black with purple undertones that shimmered in the light when she moved. The suit crept up her neck, stopping in a crisp line under her nose, all the way around her head. Across her eyes appeared a black band as if she were looking at them from the gate of the underworld, brought to this place to show them the way. The white streak in her hair disappeared as her hair swept up the sides of her head, creating a black plume like a horse's tail. She knew the transformation had had the desired effect when she smelled urine wafting in her direction.

She pushed her left leg back, anchoring her foot perpendicular to her hips, bending her knee to ninety degrees to drop her pelvis and lower her center of gravity. Lifting her arms and opening her chest, she looked down at her armband. Seeing the symbol shaped in the same way as her body was lit up, she opened herself to flow.

She focused on her target, the man just beyond her fingers, with the intensity of an owl hunting a field mouse. Sending white-hot light orbs from her hand, she blew a hole the size of her fist through his face. His head exploded in a cloud of blood and viscera.

The soldiers around her didn't have time to fully comprehend the true threat she posed. Flowing with the Ballet of Breath, she moved her body to hit every soldier with deadly efficiency. Her armband gave her the energies she stored there for such occasions. She called on flexibility to move in a greater range. Warrior called on protector, provider and teacher. She bent, flowed, and feigned, allowing inspiration to thunder through her, maximizing her movements and letting the light do the work. If it hadn't been a massacre, the light show would have been spectacular.

She eliminated the threat in the blink of an eye. Sinking down on one knee, she rested her head on her other knee, which bent into her chest. The air was full of bloody mist that would take a minute to settle, coating the forest in a thin red blanket.

As the normal forest sounds returned, she lifted her head and took in the carnage around her. She had intended to make their deaths as painless as possible, so she had blown their heads off or incinerated large portions of their bodies. She had moved so fast and with such precision that some of the men's lower bodies stood in boots like bizarre sentinels on their last watch, their guts making plopping sounds as they slid to the ground. The crows would eat well that day.

She walked through the bloodbath looking for supplies and a sword for Luke. He needed to learn how to use one, and she would teach him. She thought the sword the blond man had carried would be suitable, so she pulled it off the tatters of his body. After collecting as much as she could carry, she jogged into the forest.

It didn't take her long to catch up with Luke. He wasn't hard to find. She could hear the horses crashing through the forest. She got ahead of him, and she was leaning against a tree as he broke into a clearing, forcing him to skid to a halt when he saw her. The horses snorted in indignation.

"How did you do that?" he asked. "And what happened back there? Are you OK?" Luke had a horrified look on his face as he jumped down from his horse.

"Of course I'm OK. Why wouldn't I be?" she replied, wiggling her eyebrows as she smiled at him.

"Well, for one thing, you're covered in blood." She had changed back to her traveling garb, and it was covered with a thin layer of gore.

"Oh, that." Ari looked down at herself as she sauntered over to her horse and her saddlebags. "None of it's mine. I'm going to clean myself up. While I'm doing that, go through the pack and organize it between the saddle bags." She motioned to the pack leaning against a tree, next to her leg. "When I get back, we'll eat and start training."

Luke just stood there watching her as she turned and walked into the forest, whistling. He wasn't sure what was going on, and he needed answers. How could someone be covered in blood and not care? What happened back there? Who was after him? Training? How was he going to fit the contents of her bag into the saddle bags? Her bag was half his size!

He bent over and took some deep breaths. This was a lot to handle, and he didn't understand what was going on. He decided to ask her to explain while they were eating.

Ari returned just as Luke was using a flint and steel to light a fire.

"Much better. It's amazing how great it feels to be clean," she said as she floated out of the forest and into the clearing.

"I'm sure," he replied, sounding much calmer than he felt. "Can you answer some questions now? I don't appreciate being left in the dark, especially since I'm the one in the middle of all of this."

"Luke, it's OK. You're OK. I'm OK. Everything is OK. Take a deep breath and ask your first question," she said as she put the pot on the fire and started a stew with some leftover rabbit they had.

Luke was a little bit taken aback. OK? Everything was not OK. Breathing deeply, he tried to decide what to ask first.

"What was that about?"

"Some men were sent to hunt you down and possibly kill you. And most likely me too."

"Why?" Luke didn't think he was special, and he was having a difficult time wondering why anyone would want to kill him.

"You are Star Born. The Light in Darkness. The One."

"What does that mean?"

"It means there's a prophecy about you that has been active for a number of years that speaks about you Bringing the Light. I don't know all the particulars, and I'm getting more information the more time we spend together."

Her casual tone infuriated him. "See? What does that even mean? 'Getting more information the more time we spend together'?" Luke threw his arms up in frustration.

"Take a deep breath. What I mean is that when we walk the path, we don't always know the exact destination. We go as far as we can see, then we can see further."

Luke found that to be oddly reassuring. "I guess that makes sense. Why did you take a sword?" He nodded to the sword that he had left leaning against the fallen tree that he was sitting on.

"Because I'm going to teach you how to use it. We can get started while the stew finishes cooking. Remember the Ballet of Breath?" she asked, unbuttoning her armband and bending it, so it would lay flat and she could read from it.

"Yes. How could I ever forget it?"

"What do you know about it?"

"It's an ancient language and practice. It was created by the light beings from the Otherside as a tool to bring ladinya into the body, allowing for alignment and movement. By shifting your body into different shapes or poses, you can create different frequencies, also known as emotions."

"Wow! Word for word. Well done. Do you know what it means?"

Luke thought for a moment. "What I observed was a consistent breath. Whatever shape you were in, you never lost your breath. And grace. It was so smooth, almost like you were doing it underwater."

"Good job! Yes, breath is the foundation and tool to move and shift ladinya. By doing the Ballet of Breath, you are calling attention to blocks, so you can bring your awareness and breath there to remove or release the blocks. This is the written language of the Ballet of Breath." She ran her fingers lovingly over the symbols on her armband. "For example, this one here." She pointed to a symbol that was an equilateral triangle without the bottom line and with one side bowed in. "It's for rejuvenation and strength. It opens the belly space, creating fire and power, and brings nutrients to the brain, among other benefits. Some of these symbols can create things like power, strength, flexibility, and balance, and if you know how to enchant this piece like I do, you can store these energies to be used later. You can also put them into sequences that can be used for creation or destruction." She paused, watching as the wheels turned in Luke's mind. "As part of my training as a Soldier of Light, I've mastered this practice and can teach it to you. It's about letting the power move through you rather than being the source of it. Finding balance in all things, knowing that if there's light, there's also dark. Life and death. And knowing which side you're on. Once you're clear about who you are and what you stand for and can move the ladinya, everything else is logistics."

Great, Luke thought. *So, all I have to do is trust the process, figure out all my values, and be able to somehow move ladinya as easily as breathing. We're doomed.*

"Luke, I see that look on your face, and it's going to be OK. I'm going to teach you what you need to know, and we'll figure out the rest. Have faith."

Luke realized he was holding his breath, so he let it out slowly through his mouth.

"Ah! There you go. You're halfway there already!" Ari exclaimed, a big smile on her face. "Where there is breath, there is life. Where there is life, there is hope. If you open your mind and your heart and work hard, you'll figure it out. And if you don't, I'll beat it into you." Ari laughed at the horrified look on Luke's face. "Let's get started."

EIGHTEEN

"As I said before, ladinya is always moving," Ari said. "One of the ways it flows is with our breath. I like to think of it as a wave that flows in and out. We can control it at times, but in truth, the breath often breathes us. It's not something we need to think of consciously because if you don't breathe, you die, but you can also use the breath as a tool to move blocks." They had finished dinner, and she was sitting cross-legged on the ground. Luke was lying prone in front of her, his face in the dirt.

"One of the most important things to remember is that your breath carries oxygen, which keeps you connected. Cutting the flow causes dispersion and dangerous, irrational acts without you realizing it until it's too late.

"Breathing through the nose causes the breath to warm and to be pushed to the bottom of the lungs, oxygenating and cleansing your body. Breathing through the mouth is cooling. I often force my breath out of my mouth when I've released some ladinya, allowing the junk to ride out of my mouth.

"Samdra is a constricted breath used to occupy the mind and allow for calming. This is the type of breath I use while I'm doing the Ballet of Breath, as I find it the most effective and efficient way to move ladinya. You can create this breath by constricting the back of your throat and creating a *haaaaaa* sound. You try."

Of course, he figured it out immediately.

"Take a deep breath in through your nose," she said after he inhaled some dirt. "Feel the ground under your body. Place your hands on the ground, the top of your shoulders lined up above your fingertips. Move them a little ... yes, right there. Splaying your hands on the ground, claw your fingertips, creating a tent with your palms, and root the knuckles at the base of your fingers. Can you feel how your arms engage? Can you feel the ladinya?" She heard a muffled "yes," so she continued. "Roll your shoulders up toward your ears and move them down your back as if you were trying to put them in the pockets on the back of your pants."

"Pockets on the back of my pants? Who puts pockets in the back of their pants? They would have to sit on anything they put back there," he said, turning his head to talk to her. A spot of dirt in the middle of his forehead made it hard for Ari to take him seriously.

"It's a figure of speech," Ari replied. That seemed to satisfy Luke, who put his forehead back on the ground.

She had been teaching him the foundations of the Ballet of Breath. There were an almost infinite number of poses, but Ari focused on the basics. At the moment she was teaching him how to engage his back.

"Breathe deeply through your nose, constricting the back of your throat." She heard the resistance of breath as his torso rose. This breath forced the air down to the bottom of his lungs, allowing him to focus on controlling his diaphragm.

"Put your shoulder blades in your back pocket," Ari said, "and tuck the bottom of your shoulder blades under. Yes, feel the opening across your chest. Take a breath there." He was exceptionally good at taking instruction, which was refreshing. The worst circumstance for Ari was an unwilling student. She firmly believed that when the student was ready, the teacher would appear, and Luke was ready.

"Take another breath, tuck your tailbone, and feel your core engage. Keep your butt relaxed, and engage your thighs, pushing them into the ground. Roll your inner thighs toward the sky. Lay the tops of your feet down and point your toes." It was so fascinating for her to watch him. As he engaged certain muscles, his aura shifted, allowing ladinya to flow where it had been stuck. It looked so natural for him.

"Engaging your back and your core, lift your head, hands, and legs off the ground. Keep your toes pointed. And breathe. This isn't as effective if you don't breathe." He had been holding his breath for so long that his face had almost turned purple.

"Excellent. Now lower to the ground." She left him like that for a few breaths, so he could process what he had just done.

"Now lay your arms down by your sides, palms up. Put your forehead back on the ground. We aren't done." He had turned his head to lie on one ear as if he were going to have a nap.

"Deep breath in, energize everything, and lift again. Yes! Pull your shoulders down, reaching back with your hands. Feel your back working and your chest opening." She knew when he found the sweet spot because he lit up. She could see the ladinya moving through his houses unobstructed. It almost danced through his body, joyful in the opportunity, a beautiful sight.

"When that feels complete, relax, resting your ear on the ground and taking a few breaths."

When he opened his eyes, they were bursting with euphoria. "How did that feel?" she asked as if she didn't already know the answer.

"That was amazing. Does it always feel like that?" He was a little breathless after the flood of happiness through his body.

"Yes, when it's done properly. Sometimes you have to work a little harder, which we'll get into when the time is right. The real trick is to use your breath to occupy your mind and allow your intuition to come through to guide your practice. I can tell you, it's easier said than done.

"The Ballet of Breath is a tool. Your thoughts"—she pointed at her temple—"and your intention"—she placed her hand over her heart—"are what matter."

When she spoke next it was like the wind blowing on a full moon: refreshing, awe-inspiring, and humbling. "If you can imagine it here"—she patted her chest—"and have this"—she pointed at her temple—"truly in alignment and clear, it has to happen."

Luke stared at her. If he understood correctly, it meant that as long as he had complete and full belief to the point of already feeling like he had achieved his goal, he could create whatever he wanted. Anything. His job was only to ask and wait while the universe created it for him.

"You got it," Ari whispered, the silence shattering like glass. She was so excited to see her student learning.

"Focus on the feeling as if it's already happened." Luke's voice matched Ari's. He looked at her, his eyes full of hope. "So, I just have to imagine peace across the land and, poof, it will happen?"

"Yes." A wave of ladinya swept down Luke's body in response to her reply, leaving a trail of goosebumps. "However, if you're inspired to take action, it's the right direction. This leverages your ladinya, minimizing waste."

Luke nodded in understanding. "But how can I create something so impossible that includes so many people?" Hopelessness had seeped back into his voice.

"There are a few reasons," she said, reigniting the spark of hope in Luke's eyes. "First, you came here with an unparalleled challenge and crystal-clear intention. You also brought more tools with you than the average person. Second, you've enlisted others who have the gifts, skills, and talents that you lack to help you toward this goal."

"How?" Luke asked. He didn't understand how he could have made people help him when he was just a baby.

"When you were still on the other side, you made soul agreements with other beings. I'm one of them. I don't know what the agreement is, but the details aren't necessary. I know I've been working my whole life to help you, and here I am."

Her breezy confidence washed over Luke, soothing his heart. He knew he couldn't do it alone, and he was comforted to hear that he had laid the groundwork to receive help, even if he didn't remember doing so.

"One of the ways to make sure you're able to receive help is to make sure you're clear. And one way to do this is the Ballet of Breath," she said, bringing the conversation full circle.

NINETEEN

rnold, High Commander of King Nadiri's roving army, used a stick to poke a dismembered leg that wore the same uniform as him. He was disappointed at what he saw. These men had been his elite team, trained by him, and it was disconcerting to see them all exploded to one degree or another, having died without even putting up a fight. They had greatly underestimated their quarry. He turned and looked at the wizard.

"What happened here?"

"My best guess is a light orb," Zion replied, tapping his chin with his finger. He had seen this before and knew it was a specific skill. The scene in front of him told him exactly what he didn't want to know.

"Light orb? What do you mean?"

"When light is focused in a precise way, it can cut through anything. Not many people can do this, and those who can are a serious threat. I have only heard of two people with such skills, and if the person I'm thinking of did this, we need to be careful. She has a number of other skills and talents that are challenging to counteract. However, I'm just as good. At least we know what we're dealing with now."

"She? Surely a woman can't be responsible for this carnage," Arnold said, motioning to all the dead soldiers around them.

"This person is more dangerous *because* she's a woman," Zion said as he scanned the road. "She has an entire dimension to her being that men lack, allowing her to tap into a power we can only imagine. Second, she is singularly focused and will stop at nothing to complete her task. She has spent her entire life mastering her skills. These skills bolster her abilities, and as a result, she is a deadly warrior with a heart of gold. We need to be careful." As he spoke of her, his voice contained a mixture of admiration and loathing. He hadn't expected Ari to be helping the boy. For the first time since he had birthed the plan, he worried it might not work.

"I'm sure if we work together, me, my men, and a wizard can take her down!" Arnold said.

"She will protect her quarry like none that you have experienced," Zion replied. "She can move through the ether up to the seventh dimension and can create what she needs, making it appear in a moment, as if pulling it from thin air. We used to call her the Alchemist, which she hated. She is not to be underestimated." Zion was annoyed that Arnold wasn't taking him seriously. Then Zion remembered that he didn't care if these men died or not, which improved his mood.

"We need to find the boy," Arnold said. "Which way did they go?"

He had sent trackers to find the trail. Just as he asked the question, a scout came out of the forest and pointed to the way he had come. "I found two separate sets of tracks. One is two horses that start a ways back, and the other is a single track. Small. Looks like a woman who was running."

Zion raised his eyebrows at Arnold as if he had won the bet. "Mount up! I want them found by sunset!"

The soldiers knew it would be their heads if they didn't find their quarry. They also knew this was a particular case and to be careful.

TWENTY

Ari stowed their bowls in her saddle bag, then cocked her head to the left as if she were listening for something. Then she sat beside the fire and made three cups of tea.

Luke watched her, brow creased with concern. Leaving the three cups of tea by the fire to steep, she took off her boots. By that point, nothing surprised Luke. He decided to throw caution to the wind and inquire anyway.

"What are you doing?"

"I'm going to make a call," Ari replied. She reached for her pack and unlaced a drum and a baton that Luke hadn't noticed before. An enormous tree was painted around one quarter of the drum's rim. It had reddish bark and needled branches from the middle to the top. As she moved the drum, a leather strip with beads and feathers knotted into it on each side jangled. She weaved her fingers through the laces in the back that held the skin taut. Rubbing the skin with affection, she offered warmth in their time of need in exchange for carrying a message. Luke was mesmerized by her treatment of the instrument, as if she were welcoming a friend into her home for food and warmth. She sat across from him, gazing over the fire.

"When you feel ready, 'ohm' this note." She drew a deep breath, her back and belly fully expanded, giving the air permission to enter and fill. Allowing the breath to fan her relaxed vocal cords, she vibrated them to septa, the seventh note of the musical scale. The sound washed over Luke, bathing him in sunlight and crackling flames, the heat gloriously warm and dry. When she finished the note, Luke realized he had closed his eyes to drink in the feeling.

"Whenever you feel ready," she said, one eyebrow raised. He nodded.

With that, she bounced the baton on the skin, producing a warm thump. She created a tattoo, following what Luke realized was the rhythm of his heartbeat. It was faster than he thought it was. As he sat with his eyes closed, inhaling the clean forest air, the drumbeat gradually slowed.

Then the beat synchronized with Mother Earth's heartbeat, and the world exploded into colors and flow. He watched ladinya move across the ground and loop up, up, and up. As he observed the flow, he realized it was a tree. A jerky movement caught his attention. He focused on the spot and saw it was a small rabbit. He looked down at himself, noticing he was a loop like the tree was. His eyes roved over the grove, noticing how everything was connected. Suddenly, he realized he wasn't in his body. Then he did the only thing he could think of to stay tethered to his body.

"Ohm," he sang, and it was glorious. He wanted to stay there forever, but one molecule of his being said, *You can't. They need you.* He acknowledged it and then brought his attention to Ari. She was stunning. Her aura was sparkling with rainbow motes, a kaleidoscope of color and light... that he had seen before. No sooner had that thought crossed his mind than Ari started singing, her voice rich and deep, sliding flawlessly between notes:

My friend,
Sage
Dirt and air
Water and tree
Light and love

Come to me
We require guidance

Luke's "ohm" finished succinctly with Ari's last note and the drumbeat. The song flew through the forest, boosted by Luke's contribution. Afterwards, they sat in silence, absorbing the electric hum that emanated through the forest.

Eventually, Luke opened his eyes, meeting Ari's gaze.

"How was that?" she asked.

"Ugh." His vocal cords were temporarily disconnected from his brain; he had done so much rewiring.

"Breathe," Ari said, holding his gaze and breathing with him.

"It was you," he managed a few minutes later. "Colors and light. It wasn't a dream; it was a memory."

She leaned over the fire, the light illuminating her saccharine smile. "Why, whatever do you mean?" she asked, though she knew exactly what he was talking about.

Before he could answer, the bush behind him rustled. As fast as Ari filled her hand with crackling yellow light, Luke stood up and spun around, drawing his sword. He was so graceful that Ari was sure she was watching a ballet dancer toe the line of physics, flawlessly blending athleticism and dance, blooming like a flower reaching toward the morning sun.

"Oh, who is this?" a willowy being said, looking him up and down as a branch moved aside.

Out of the forest stepped an entity who looked like a human-shaped tree. Blue tattoo lines starting at their temples extended above their eyebrows, under their eyes, and across their cheeks to the edges of their mouth. One line bisected their chin. Standing a head taller than Luke, the figure was so slim, Luke figured a stiff wind could blow them away.

As the being strode past Luke, he noticed they had brown eyes and dark brown hair woven with lichens and moss, mimicking tree bark. The figure blended into the forest so well that Luke was pretty sure he wouldn't have noticed them standing directly in front of him had they not made a noise.

Ari leapt up and embraced the being in a deep hug. "Hello, Sage. It's so good to see you. Thank you for coming."

"My pleasure," Sage said as they pulled away. "I happened to be in the area, and I'm so happy to see you. It's been too long. How may I be of service?" The being's voice was deep and smooth like the beat of an oak tree's heart.

"Please sit and share our fire, and tell me the news of the forest."

"Thank you," Sage said, taking the cup of tea that had been steeping by the fire. "The forest speaks of turmoil. The time of light and peace is over, and darkness and war are here. I have come from the other side of the mountains where the land has been burned from the horizon right to the edge of the mountain range. As far as I could tell, the only reason the mountains weren't breached is because almost no one lives there, so there's nothing to take. It looks like whoever is doing this is looking to rape and pillage to gain land and titles. The thing is, he's killing his own people, which doesn't make sense to me. I watched from a ledge at the edge of the mountains as they rode into the town and laid waste. They took the women, killed all the men and children who weren't old enough to work, then set everything on fire, burning it to the ground." They spoke with a haunted melancholy that broke Ari's heart.

"Who is this?" Sage nodded to Luke with their chin, breaking the tension.

"That's him," Ari said, twitching her eyebrows.

"Ohhhh… well done. How's training coming along?" Sage asked as they eyed Luke up and down.

Luke was a little insulted that the two of them were talking about him as if he wasn't there.

"Excuse me. I can speak for myself."

"My apologies," Sage said, looking into his eyes. Luke felt like he was looking at a rock face after it had been warmed by the sun. Intricate, warm, and enormous beyond comprehension. "You're right. My apologies. How is your training going?"

"Uh... training. Good?" Luke's tongue felt like it was stuck to the roof of his mouth, and he found it difficult to form sentences.

"You don't sound so sure," Sage replied.

Ari burst into laughter in response to Luke's uneasiness. Seeing him speak with one of the Earth Walkers was quite entertaining, and she hadn't had a good belly laugh in weeks.

Sage hitched a thumb at Luke and looked at Ari. "Looks like you got your work cut out for you with this one."

"You have no idea," Ari replied between gasping breaths.

"What's the matter with you two?" Luke demanded. "You're sitting here like there isn't someone out there trying to capture and maybe kill me, like you don't even care. And you're laughing at me like we're old drinking buddies." Luke leapt up, pacing back and forth, his fists at his sides.

"Luke, calm down," Ari said. "No one is close to us. If there was, Sage would have heard them from the forest, and we would be taking action. It's important to take one moment at a time and be thankful this moment is a peaceful one."

Sucking in a deep breath through his nose, Luke continued to pace, muttering to himself. Spinning, he pointed a finger in Sage's face. "Who are you?"

"He asks that a lot," Ari said to Sage, as if trying to tell them not to take Luke's question personally.

Sage opened their mouth to answer when something caught their attention, and they averted their eyes into the forest behind Luke. The moment Sage's focus shifted to over his shoulder, Luke threw his Senses in that direction, forming a pulse wave that was tethered to the golden egg in which he was suddenly encased. It wasn't so much that he had to force his energy out in pulsating waves; it was that he had to release the restraint of his birthright. It had always been a part of him, and now, with Ari's help, that part of him had awakened. The pulses came back to him like sonar, and he knew how many men, what weapons they were carrying, and the direction they were coming from. Of course, this was only some of the information he had sifted from the enormous amount of feedback he'd received. He didn't need to register that the closest man was nursing a lung infection due to the missing top button on his coat. Besides, it wouldn't matter because his jacket would soon be on a dead man.

In the next moment, having all the information he needed, Luke created a plan for how to annihilate the threat. Without hesitation, he twisted around while drawing his sword. Luke swung his sword diagonally, from groin to shoulder, through the person who would have taken off his head. On the downswing, he sliced through the shoulder of an assailant on his other side and then across, slicing the man in front of him in half. He did all of this instinctively, and by the time his mind realized what he was doing, he had already cut down the next man. By then mayhem had erupted in the camp, and all three were fighting for their lives.

Ari knew Luke had the gift to be a deadly swordsman, but her jaw still dropped when she stole a glance over her shoulder and saw him in motion. He wasn't fighting as much as he was dancing. He was a picture of grace and poise, flexibility and power, strength and vulnerability. His blade was a silver blur of lightning as bodies piled up around him. Every movement had a purpose, and he did no more and no less than what was needed to follow through. She also noticed a golden egg around him, and she knew that as long as she walked with him on the path, everything would be OK. She would think more about that later. Right now, she was locked in a deadly battle with an entity in the forest.

It had come straight for her; she had felt it as soon as she loosened her Senses. At the same time Luke had drawn his sword, she had spun on her knee, throwing her palms straight out from her chest and creating a white light shield. She expanded it to protect her and her companions. She held steady as lightning strikes assaulted it, causing sweat to break on Ari's brow as she dissipated the huge amounts of energy by absorbing them and shifting them into sound waves, causing boom after boom to rock the forest. It looked like a vibrant lightning show that illuminated the immediate area. It would have been dazzling had it not been a fight to the death. Because of the ease with which her assailant was able to channel the light, she knew exactly who it was. She also knew he didn't have a connection to the earth like Sage did.

While Ari held her assailant behind her shield of light, Sage waved their arms as if conducting an orchestra. In time to music only Sage could hear, tree branches moved to defend against their attackers. They swung in great arcs, sweeping the ground with deadly force and tossing men through the air. Ari heard the men's screams dissipate as they disappeared into the darkness. When they noticed Ari holding her shield of light, they gathered all their power to bring down the branch over the assailant's head. Unfortunately, they weren't fast enough. There was a crack, as if from a whip, and a bolt of black lightning struck the branch as it fell, incinerating it into a cloud of ash. With the lightning came a concussion that Ari was barely able to deflect, dissipating the energy back into the forest and away from the camp using her shield.

The silence was deafening. Ari dropped her light shield as the dust settled, putting her hand on the ground for support while she caught her breath. When she lifted her head, she looked over at Luke, who was standing in a circle of bodies, his sword dripping with blood.

"Is everyone OK?" Sage asked, looking back and forth between their two companions.

"Yes," Ari replied as she stood. "Luke?"

He was shaking, his knuckles white on his sword hilt. But his eyes were filled with a quiet peace that turned them a dark metallic royal purple. He blinked a few times as he regained his breath, relaxing his stance.

"What happened? All I remember is asking Sage who they were," he said, looking around in confusion.

Sage and Ari exchanged a look. They both noted that Luke's eyes had changed to a unique color seen on only one other person.

"You don't remember killing all those men? Defending yourself?" Ari asked, nodding to the twenty dead men in an almost perfect circle a sword's length away around his legs. "This is excellent!" she said, clapping her hands and jumping up and down with delight.

"Well done, sister! This is wonderful!" Sage said, joining in the celebration.

Luke cleaned his sword, sheathed it, and then bent over, catching his breath. When he straightened up, he realized his companions were eyeing him expectantly.

"What?" Luke asked, looking between the two.

"We unlocked a gift!" Ari exclaimed. "I saw it in you, and we just needed the right circumstances to pull it out. Now I can train you to stay present while entranced, and you'll be the whole package."

Luke couldn't believe his eyes. He had killed twenty men and didn't even remember doing it? He was a monster. If this was what being a leader meant, he didn't want any part of it. The thought must have shown on his face.

"Luke, you had to defend yourself," Ari said. "You have to stand up for yourself because no one else will. If you see an injustice, it's your duty to step in. And know you have all the support because you have the right intention. If you are spreading light, there can be no darkness."

Ari walked toward Luke and put her hands on his shoulders, looking into his eyes. What she saw there was what she had been looking for since they'd first met. King Luke. Protector of the people. Light in the dark. He had arrived.

When Luke looked up, Sage dropped to their right knee and crossed their right arm across their chest as a salute. Sage felt blessed to witness this moment, as it was what they had been waiting for. After seeing what was on the other side of the mountains, Sage had worried the world was destined for a time of great darkness. As they had worked their way back across the mountain range, Sage was hopeful that someone was on the way. And then the forest had told Sage that Ari needed guidance. Sage had no idea it was for something so significant. When Sage lifted their head, Ari was standing up after her own salute.

"We need to go. Sage, lead the way."

TWENTY-ONE

Luke wasn't sure what was going on, but he felt different, like a veil had been lifted or some part of him had been uncovered. He felt a deeper connection with himself, to a power that had always been there; he just needed to tap into it. He knew he could trust his new teachers and protectors, and he was excited to learn everything he could from them.

They picked up what they could salvage from the camp, found their horses, and then continued on their way.

"How do you think they snuck up on us?" Ari asked Sage once they slowed to give the horses a rest. "You said the forest told you that no one was around."

"According to my sources, no one was. They must have had some type of cloaking spell. What attacked you? They must have been the one to do it."

"Cloaking spell? Is this magic?" Luke inquired.

"Yes," Ari replied. "Some people have a level of intensity, power, and gifts that qualifies them as a wizard. Wizards can be men or women, and they are born with their power. You can learn new skills, but you must be born with power. I know who that was back there, and we are evenly matched, so that's good to know."

"Was it you-know-who?" Sage asked, knowing it was a touchy subject for Ari.

"His name is Wizard Sloan, Zion, the Second of His Name, Light Born of the Third House," Ari replied with a deep breath that told of sadness and regret.

"If you are equally matched, does that mean you're a wizard too?" Luke asked. "I didn't think wizards would be Soldiers of Light."

"Since I was a young girl, I have been training in using my powers, and when the time came, I decided to become a Soldier of Light, so I could be of service. My time studying at the Citadel came to an end, so I chose a different path. Some of the people I grew up with, trained with, and who supported me felt like I was turning my back on the art of wizardry, something no one does. So, they disowned me because I chose this life of service, study, and practice. I figured because my calling is to help others walk the path, being a Path Walker as a Soldier of Light was a better fit. And here I am."

"Was that wizard one of the people you grew up with?" Luke asked. "Trained with?"

"Yes. He and I were best friends growing up. He wanted a more intimate relationship, and apparently, he took my choice of this life harder than I thought. He always had darkness in him, and my guess is that someone is supporting him in making dark choices."

"Is he the one who's after me?" Luke asked, pulling his horse up next to Ari's as the path widened.

"He is definitely one of the people who's after you. I'm aware of one other, and they could be working with someone else as a trio, but I don't think so."

"How can you do that?"

"Do what?"

"Talk as if you know everything will work out? You don't know everything, so how can you know it's going to be OK?"

"Luke, everything will be OK in the end. If it's not OK, it's not the end."

Luke didn't know what to make of that.

"What does Light Born of the Third House mean?" he asked.

Ari sighed. "Light Born means we naturally have some ability to control ladinya in the form of light, or laghu." She pronounced "lag" with an up note and "hu" lower and more abrupt. "'Laghu' means 'little light' in the ancient language. My special gifts focus on healing and light orbs, with a smattering of other things. Zion can move like lightning by harnessing the ladinya in the ether, using it as fuel to raise his vibration enough to travel on the laghu in the environment. It might sound cool, but that's the only thing he can do. Well, other than the basics. He could have learned more, but he's never moved through the third house.

"The talent to manipulate laghu expresses itself differently in every person, and discovering and uncovering its true abilities and power is a lifelong journey. The houses are centers of ladinya in the human body, each one corresponding to a color, organs, characteristics, and challenges. House seven is the highest number—well, that any human has achieved."

"How common is it once you get to the higher numbers?" Luke asked.

Sage gave Ari a sidelong glance. This wasn't common knowledge, but they knew Ari felt it was safe to share it with him. Sage had been a close friend of Ari's for many years, and they only ever heard her mention this information once.

"I've only ever heard of four people who achieved house seven."

"Oh. In your lifetime?"

"No. In all of history."

Luke gulped. "Are you Light Born? I've seen some of those talents you didn't want to share with me, and I've never seen anyone do what you do."

Ari puffed out a despondent sigh. "Yes. I am Light Born of the Seventh House."

Luke let out a low whistle. He realized he shouldn't be surprised by anything Ari told him anymore. He decided to throw caution to the wind. "Is there anything else I should know about you? Do you have any other secret abilities?"

"You could tell him your name," Sage suggested, smiling at Ari and batting their eyelashes.

"I suppose I could. Although it's not really relevant," Ari replied, scowling. She hadn't shared her full title with Luke because she didn't want to intimidate him. But if her title scared him, he wasn't who she thought he was.

"My name is Wizard Arulea, Ariella, the First of Her Name, Light Born of the Seventh House, She Who Transcends, Healer, Namer, Path Walker." As she shared her name, a soap-like bubble engulfed her, illuminating the space around them with shimmering rainbows, almost making Luke shield his eyes. When she finished, it dimmed and died out.

"That's a mouthful," Luke said. "I almost fell asleep. No wonder you don't want to tell people." They all burst into jovial laughter at the unexpected reaction. It released some of the tension after the battle.

"Sage, how long will it take us to get across the mountains?" Ari asked, hoping to change the subject.

"Well, it's summer, so that's a big help. A few weeks if we make good time. Unfortunately, we'll have to leave the horses and go on foot soon, as it's too treacherous in places."

"OK. Lead the way!"

With that, Sage spurred their horse, and they rode in the light of the full moon.

TWENTY-TWO

When the sun had crested in the sky, they stopped their horses and dismounted. They had finally reached the foot of the mountain pass after being able to see it for two days. They had been riding hard, practically living in the saddle, and Luke was looking forward to making camp and getting some sleep. They retrieved their belongings from the saddle bags, and after Ari thanked each horse with a scratch behind the ear and an apple, she released them with a slap on the rump.

Sage was an expert mountain guide. Being nomadic, they lived and thrived in that land and had been on the move their entire life. Ari had been across the mountains a few times but never with this type of urgency. She was also glad it was summer. The snow and ice made some of the passes impassable at times during the winter, and going around them was not a luxury they had.

They were making good time when they decided to stop and camp. As they had been in the saddle for the past two days straight, it was heavenly to be back on the ground. They were exhausted and were looking forward to some much-needed rest. Sage rolled out their bedroll beside the fire and fell asleep as soon as they were done eating. Sage was going to take the middle watch, and they wanted to catch up on some rest before they were woken up in the middle of the night. This gave Ari and Luke privacy to talk about what had happened over the last few days.

"I understand what's going on a little better now," Luke said. "I feel like something is different in me. Not that I've learned something new, more like I've uncovered something I've always had."

"That's good to hear. You feel that way because that's exactly what happened. The truth is that you already have everything inside that you need to achieve what you came here to do. An age-old prophecy speaks of a prince raised by peasants to be the one to light the darkness. It also states that this man was born of noble blood but adopted outside the kingdom because of the wars that would happen due to his birth and swift death. His parents, King Gurham and Queen Shanti, who were aware of this prophecy, understood the threat of keeping him in their kingdom, the place he had a right to rule, after he was attacked when he was only minutes old. It was the hardest decision they ever made, but they knew it was the only option. Queen Shanti did not rise from her bed for twenty-one days afterward, and it took much ministering of light healing to help her. I don't think she will ever fully recover. Although she may if she sees you before she passes."

Again, Luke couldn't believe it. He was a prince? There was a kingdom out there that technically belonged to him? He was a born protector of the people? Ari knew his parents? His ma and pa weren't his birth parents? It was overwhelming.

"You know my mother? The queen?" Luke whispered, trying not to break down sobbing. He knew in his heart that everything Ari had told him was true.

"Yes. Queen Shanti is the most beautiful woman I have ever served. It's not her piercing metallic purple eyes or her dark cascading hair that make her beautiful. It's the light of peace that shines from her heart, making her eyes sparkle. She is so committed to the peace of their kingdom and the safety of their people that she sent you away to avoid a possible war. If you were killed, her king, your father, would have avenged your death by starting a war. So, not only would you, her only son, be dead, they would be in the middle of costly and unnecessary wars at the expense of their subjects, just after achieving peace. It wasn't something she was willing to take on or ask her people to do. So, she sent you away. You have her eyes, by the way. Well, since you stepped into your power a few days ago."

Ari took a deep breath and rolled her shoulders to release the tension that she had been holding there. This had been a heavy burden, and she felt lighter now that she was able to tell him the truth. He wouldn't have believed Ari until he had experienced some of what they had been though. She wasn't sure he believed her now.

"My heart is telling me your words are true. It answers a few questions I've had, explains some emotions I've felt, and some recurring dreams I've had over my lifetime. I always felt like I was destined for greatness. I just didn't know what it was or how it looked. I guess that was my pure blood talking to me."

Ari looked at Luke, wide eyed. He was a blood listener too! She shouldn't have been so surprised. He came from two lineages that had an assortment of gifts and talents. It wouldn't be shocking if he had inherited a number of special talents.

"Is there anything else?" Luke asked, rolling his eyes, as he thought that surely there couldn't be.

Locking eyes with him, Ari peered into his soul. "Your birth name is Prince Jaya, the First of His Name, Star Born, Prince of the Seven Kingdoms." Then she lowered her voice. "'Jaya' means victory in your native tongue."

A shiver rippled from the top of his head to the tips of his toes, the hairs on the back of his neck standing on end. That was it, the missing piece. He sat up straighter as if accepting his destiny. At that moment, the clouds parted, bathing Luke's face in moonlight and reminding Ari of a moment long ago.

"Call me Jaya from now on," he said, his eyes having transformed into glowing purple orbs. "Luke is no more."

"As you wish, my liege," Ari said, her fist over her heart and her head bowed.

TWENTY-THREE

They were finishing a dinner of trout from a nearby stream with roasted root vegetables that Sage had dug up. Jaya had the first watch. When the sun dipped behind the peaks, he stood up and walked out of the fire light and found a rock to perch on. After a short time, he heard Ari wish Sage a restful sleep, followed by gentle snoring.

Jaya ... Jaaayyyaaa ...

As the sound of his name tickled his senses, he almost wasn't sure he'd heard it.

Jaaaaaaaaaaaaaaaaaaaaaaayyyyyyyyyyyaaaaaaaaaaaaaaaaaaaaaaaaaa, the wind sighed.

He was instantly aware of everything around him. As they hiked through the mountains, Ari and Sage had taught him about ladinya and intuition. He had been practicing throwing his Senses at will, experimenting with what he could pick up out of the environment. He opened his eyes and scanned the area in front of him.

Jaaaaayyyyaaaa

Jaya looked to his left and saw two blue orbs and a cascade of silver hair through the trees. The figure was tall and slim and had its arm raised, waving for Jaya to follow.

He slid off the rock, his focus fixed on the figure. As he crept toward the misty shape, it moved away from him, as if leading him. Out of curiosity, he followed the shadow, moving farther away from camp. It led him through the stream, and he hopped across rocks to keep dry. Then it crossed a moonlit clearing to a cave on the other side.

As Jaya drew closer to the cave, he noticed a soft, pulsing white light coming from inside. At that moment, he realized the shadow that had been leading him was nowhere to be found. He approached the cave with caution, not wanting to come face to face with a mountain lion or a bear. Once he assured himself that it was empty, he went inside.

Deep in the cave, he discovered that the light was emanating from an altar in the middle of a pool. The longer he looked at it, the more the light shifted from white to purple. When it stopped shifting colors, settling on a deep purple, he moved to the pool and squatted by the water's edge. As he gazed at his reflection, he realized the light from the altar was the same color as his eyes. He knew it wasn't a coincidence. He also noticed his face was more angular, more mature than he remembered, and that he was in bad need of a haircut.

He walked around the pool to the back of the cave and noticed a path connecting the edge of the pool and the altar. He walked the path to the altar, testing his steps along the way. When he reached the altar, he realized the light was coming from a sword and not the altar itself. The bottom of the sword's hilt was at eye level, and he noticed writing on both sides. "Bringer" was wrought in gold. Between the cross guard and the pommel was the torso of an angel, its wings open and its arms reaching toward the pommel. In the angel's forehead was a purple, thumbnail-sized jewel that served as the door to the bearer's soul. The pommel, which acted as a counterbalance, bore a diamond the size of a robin's egg, held in place by a gold ring.

He reached out and gripped the sword, and the hilt fit perfectly in his hand, as if it had been designed for him. He tugged on it, and the broad sword came free with a ring like the tolling of a bell.

The sound reverberated around the cave while Jaya held the sword above his head, throwing pulsing purple light that bounced around the cave and reflected off the water. Waves of light flowed down the blade, over his body to the ground, and back up, as if the sword were vetting him. It must have approved because the light waves concentrated in his chest, making their home in his heart.

Once the vibrations dissipated and the light dimmed, Jaya examined the blade. It was beautifully balanced and sharper than any he had ever seen. But what fascinated him was its color. He watched as deep metallic purple seeped from his hand, through the angel, and up the blade. He didn't know that this only happened when Light Bringer was held by the one for whom it had been forged. It had never been that color before.

After swinging it and getting a feel for it, he concluded that the blade had been forged for him, though he didn't know when or by whom or how it had come to be in the cave. Perhaps Ari or Sage knew. As he scanned the cave one last time before heading back, he saw something leaning against the altar he was sure hadn't been there before. It was a pristine white scabbard etched in ancient symbols similar to the ones on Ari's armband. Between the etched symbols were colored circles. The bottom circle, almost at the tip of the scabbard, was red. It was created by chips of red crystals placed in concentric circles that almost touched the outside edges. Above that was an identical circle, except in orange. A yellow circle was above that and a green one above that. Just under the hilt was a blue circle.

He threw the baldric over his head, then slid the sword into the scabbard, which rested perfectly on his hip. Then he turned away from the altar and hurried out of the cave and back to camp.

When he got close, he could hear Ari and Sage talking.

Why are they still up? he wondered as he splashed through the creek.

"Jaya! There you are! What's going on?" Ari was glad to see him safe. They had both been woken by a sound, though neither of them could pinpoint what it was or where it came from. As Ari examined Jaya, she noticed the hilt of the sword was not the one she had given him. The scabbard and baldric were different too.

"What are you wearing?" Ari asked with a slightly threatening tone.

"I was sitting on the rock over there standing watch when I heard the wind breathing my name. I looked up and saw a figure with silver hair cascading down its back and two blue orbs. I didn't know who or what it was, but my gut told me to follow it. I was led to a cave where this sword was in an altar in the middle of a pool. When I gripped the hilt, which fit perfectly into my hand, and pulled it out, I heard the tolling of a bell. I also noticed the blade is the same color as my eyes."

Jaya was confused by the look on Ari and Sage's faces. They had moved from concern to distrust to understanding and acceptance in the blink of an eye.

"It is truly time, sister," Sage said reverently, looking at Ari.

"We are further along in the flow of time than I was hoping," Ari said as she began to pace. "Although this is a good thing. I mean, he found Light Bringer. Or Light Bringer found him, I suppose."

"What's the matter, sister?" Sage asked as Ari continued to pace, wringing her hands. "You knew this was going to happen."

"Yes. I suppose I did. Can I see the blade?" Ari asked, her demeanor shifting to acceptance.

Jaya drew the sword from the scabbard. As soon as the blade moved, the gentle sound of a bell tolling swept over them as purple light illuminated the forest. Jaya looked at the sword in wonder. It felt like an extension of his arm, as if it were a piece of his heart, held outside his body.

As soon as the thought crossed his mind, the light shifted from purple to pink, and a gentle hum filled the air. As he lowered the sword, he realized Ari and Sage were kneeling before him.

"Please stand up," he said. "It's super weird that you two do that."

Ari rose to her feet. "Well, you may want to get used to it, Prince Jaya. However, if it is your wish, Sage and I will only salute with our hands on our hearts."

"That is my wish."

"So be it," Ari replied with a nod.

Jaya slid Light Bringer into the scabbard, extinguishing the gentle hum and the purple light. "What do you know of this sword? When and by whom was it made?"

"Before I answer that question, let's have some tea," Ari said.

When they had settled in, she began her story. "In an age before time was written, there was a Master Smith. He had shoulders like an ox and dark, intelligent, deep-set eyes. He had been studying the ways of blacksmithing for almost a millennium, like his father before him and his father before him. One day, he was working in his shop when a woman approached. She was regal and slim, her dress swirling around her legs as if there was a breeze he couldn't feel. The smith was captivated by her piercing blue eyes and knew in his heart that all his practice, training, and studying—and that of his ancestors before him—had led to that moment.

"Master Smith, my name is Apala, and it's time for us to commission the greatest sword ever forged. You already know what to do, and I will be working with you. Let's get started."

Together they worked for forty days and forty nights. They did trial after trial, to no avail. Then, on the fortieth night, as the blade was plunged into the hardening fluid, the great tolling of a bell reverberated across the land. It even echoed across the sea. The people of the town reported a black shadow and then a great white light emanating from the smith's workshop.

After the sword was quenched, the smith put the blade on the anvil, and the sword cracked in half, as if it was supposed to be two blades from the beginning. Unbeknownst to Apala and the smith, they had been forging two swords that would be known as Light Bringer and Light Taker.

"Light Taker was as dark as the devil's heart, with a matte-black blade that swallowed the light. Apala could feel the threat to the human race radiating from its blade and its black leather scabbard, so she took Light Taker to the vault in the heavens, where it remained. The first time I saw it was in a dream the night before I met you, Jaya." She looked at him from under her brow and saw him gulp. "Light Bringer chooses its bearer, turning a deep metallic purple when wielded by the one who will bring the light. And, as you've already experienced, the color of light responds to what you are feeling in your heart. Light Bringer was given to those who were chosen and then passed down. From chosen to chosen, warrior to warrior. Then, a few lifetimes before mine, it disappeared. There were many theories as to what happened to it. Some say it was stolen for safekeeping. Others said it was put in the vault beside Light Taker on the Otherside. Until it found you tonight, it hadn't been seen for almost five thousand years."

Ari had been looking straight into Jaya's eyes, unblinking. When she finished her story, Jaya took a deep breath and looked away.

"Why did it choose me?" he asked.

"Because you are the one. The prophesied one. The one to save us all. But remember, Light Bringer is a tool. An incredibly powerful tool but a tool nonetheless. You have everything you need inside you already."

Jaya knew that everything Ari had told him was true. It was time.

TWENTY-FOUR

"Oh, my love," Ari moaned.

"Mmmm…" Owen was so wrapped up in Ari that he couldn't remember his name. They were meeting between worlds, as they often did, melding until they were almost one entity. They had met at an assembly at the Citadel where Ari was still training, and Owen sat down next to her at a seminar. She had been talking to a friend, but when she felt him sit, she turned to introduce herself. From that moment, they knew they would be together until the end of their days. They had never questioned or doubted it. The first time he locked eyes with her, Owen said he had known she was the one who would hold and protect his heart until they both perished.

One reason why their bond was so strong was because they supported each other in opening the fourth house. This was the house that lived in the heart space, and they needed their relationship to experience not only the love and acceptance that is true love but also the trials and tribulations. Due to the nature of their work, they weren't able to see each other in the physical world often, so, being Light Born, they would transcend and meet between worlds.

"Where are you?" Ari inquired as she held his head to her chest and stroked his face.

"Home. Well, right now I'm with you," he replied, nuzzling his face into her chest.

"We're heading through the Tough Plains. You should join us.

We can use all the help we can get. Well, if Tora agrees, I suppose," Ari said with a knowing chuckle.

"I'm sure she'll want to join you. She loves you."

Owen's spirit slammed back into his body, making him take a deep, sharp inhale of breath before opening his eyes. He leapt out of bed, throwing the covers aside and stumbling to his bedroom door. Wrenching it open, he regained his balance and ran to the balcony railing that overlooked the great hall.

"Tora? Tora! Gear up. We're going to go meet up with Ari!"

He saw Tora lounging by the hearth, eating. Before she could make a smart remark, he ran back into his room and got dressed in his traveling clothes, stuffing the few items into his pack that had spilled out when he'd thrown it in the corner. By the time he was dressed, packed, and heading downstairs, Tora was also geared up and ready to go.

"I'm ready, my liege. Where are we off to?" she inquired, giving him a sidelong glance as she walked beside him.

"The Tough Plains to meet up with Ari. It shouldn't take long to get there."

"OK. I've packed our rations. Have you packed all your things? Did you bring your toothbrush?"

"Would you stop it?" Owen growled. He hated when she brought up such things.

"Well, you forgot it last time, so I thought I'd make sure that didn't happen again. Especially if you're going to be seeing Ari. You want to have fresh breath."

"Shut up. She won't care."

"Says you. She's the one that has to kiss you. Although I guess if she's OK with it, I should be too."

Such exchanges were typical of Owen and Tora's relationship. That didn't mean they didn't annoy Owen. He hated being treated like a child, but there wasn't a thing he could do about it. Tora considered him to be like a little brother, and a little brother's role was to put up with whatever torment his "big sister" dished out.

Tora and Owen lived in the north in a castle that had been gifted to them by the dwarves. It had been carved by masters out of the side of the mountain. The way the halls were designed kept the cold at bay. What bothered most people about it, Owen and Tora enjoyed. They loved it for its isolation, which provided breaks between when they served. It was also in a fairly central location, allowing them to travel most of the continent easily if need be, and they didn't mind the cold, crisp air, as they knew how to dress for it. Plus, when Ari visited, Owen was never cold.

Owen's auburn hair was long, curling to his shoulders and almost getting caught in his beard, which touched his chest. His speckled green-and-yellow eyes sparkled beneath heavy brows, and he looked intimidating, until he smiled. He was rumored to be able to charm a girl out of her panties with merely a smile. Even though there was no truth to it, he didn't deny it.

He wore a wolf mantle across his shoulders, which added to his abnormally tall stature. Under his cloak he wore a heavy fur-lined leather jacket, and on his feet were sturdy boots that came up to his knees.

As they walked through the castle's halls, the temperature dropped until they reached the outer courtyard, where their breath created misty clouds. They double checked, making sure their kit was secure, then mounted up and started the journey south.

TWENTY-FIVE

A cloaked and hooded figure stood in the middle of a noise-less clearing illuminated by the full moon. Fog rolled around his legs as he turned in a circle, noting the different sizes of trees around the perimeter. When he came full circle, the roots of the trees in front of him started shifting and lifting out of the ground. They gathered and gained height, forming into a man who stood eye to eye with the hooded figure. The man of roots had a beard of dark moss that matched his hair, which hung halfway down his back. His body was made of intertwined roots and branches, and he wore a cloak of leaves composed of multiple textures and colors. His eyes were dark, swirling knots.

When he finished forming from the forest floor, he lifted one gnarled hand and, with a crooked finger, moved to poke the figure on his chest, over his heart. When they touched, a spark of golden light erupted from the tree man's hand, connecting them with a lightning bolt.

The tree-man retracted his hand, pulling a ball of pulsing golden light out of the figure's heart. With the ball of energy floating in the palm of his hand, the roots lifted off the ground and became his legs, creating the illusion that he was gliding. He arrived at the foot of an enormous tree that had grown horizon-tally and then eroded, creating steps in the trunk.

As the tree-man reached the top of the stairs and proceeded closer to the trunk where it was vertical, the bark shifted and opened, revealing a cavern that was the perfect size and shape for a sword. The figure watched as the tree-man worked the ball of light with both hands, elongating it and molding it into the shape of Light Bringer. When he was done, he placed the sword of light into the tree, tip down. As soon as the tree-man released the sword, the bark closed around it. In the blink of an eye, the tree-man was once again standing eye to eye with the cloaked figure. The tree-man raised his warped finger to his lips, indicating the figure should keep quiet about what it had observed. Then he reached under the figure's hood, winked, and poked the figure between his eyes.

"Ah! Whoa! Hey!" Jaya thrashed in his bedroll, still half in the dream realm.

"Jaya! It's OK. Wake up. You're safe," a reassuring voice said. "Take a breath. There you go. What happened?"

"Oh. Uh... I had a dream. But it's OK now. I just came back abruptly, so I freaked out a bit." Jaya leaned back on his hands. He didn't want to talk about what he had seen, as he wasn't sure himself.

"I'm going to go for a walk, clear my head," he said, standing up and stepping between Ari and Sage. The sun was just peeking over the horizon, so he didn't feel too bad about having woken them up. Ari and Sage watched him walk away, concerned looks on their faces.

When he was far enough from their camp that major vibrations wouldn't be picked up, he drew Light Bringer. Except it wasn't wholly Light Bringer. It looked the same, but when he tuned into it to see if it felt the same, it did not. It felt like a piece was missing, a small piece but a piece nonetheless. No one would know, and it was still a deadly weapon. Initially, he was alarmed and angry that the tree-man had taken the liberty of separating him from part of his sword without his permission, but after a moment of contemplation, he realized there must have been a reason. He knew through the teachings he had received that no one knew everything, and there had to be a poignant reason for what had happened. Besides, he had witnessed old, powerful magic, so it must have been for a higher cause. And he couldn't do anything about it at the moment anyway.

As he made his way back to camp, he decided not to tell the others about it. His relationship with Light Bringer was his business alone—or so he thought.

TWENTY-SIX

King Nadiri was striding down the hall, his chest puffed out, his arms held a little too far from his sides, and his head tilted back to give the illusion he was looking down his nose at others. He thought it was a swagger, but he looked ridiculous because he couldn't get the timing of the walk right, resulting in a disconnected, jerky gait.

The guards standing outside the library pushed open the double doors for him. He crossed the threshold and stood in a sunbeam that clouded over as soon as he approached the middle of the room, the darkness blanketing him in shadow. He didn't notice.

"Zion. Zion!" he bellowed. "I know you're here. Don't try to hide from me. I'll find you! Where are you?" His voice rang through the air.

Zion was deep in the stacks to the king's right. At the king's first word, Zion's shoulders slumped in exasperation, and he rolled his eyes, pinching the bridge of his nose with his forefinger and thumb. As Nadiri finished his tirade, Zion made it to the banister and looked down at him.

"I am here, Your Majesty. How may I be of service?"

"Come down here. I want answers."

Zion bowed his head in understanding, then started toward the small spiral staircase tucked in the back corner. Nadiri tapped his foot impatiently until Zion was close enough to pepper with questions.

"I demand to know why nothing has happened. I could be out plundering right now. You're wasting my time, and it's not

OK." His fists were clenched at his sides.

Zion took a deep breath, lest he accidentally smite the king in anger. King Nadiri was beginning to wear on his patience, and if it wasn't for the food, drink, and women, Zion wouldn't have stayed in the castle. He figured if he had to wait for the right timing anyway, he might as well be comfortable, and dealing with the man-child was a small price to pay.

"The timing must be just right, and it's not time yet. So, I've taken this opportunity to enjoy your hospitality." He nudged the king with his elbow and wiggled his eyebrows, suggesting explicit details. The king wasn't impressed. "And I've used your library to prepare. Don't mistake my lack of activity for laziness or incompetence." A threat was threaded through Zion's voice.

King Nadiri tipped his head back to look down his nose at Zion, revealing the boogers caught in his nose hairs. Nadiri wasn't the best at grooming. It took all of Zion's calming tools not to incinerate the king where he stood. He knew it was almost time, but he couldn't tell Nadiri his plans, lest he think he could do it without Zion.

"What are you doing here?" King Nadiri asked.

"I'm studying, making sure I know as much as possible before moving forward. I am humbled by Your Majesty's library and have found volumes that I have never encountered before, which is no easy feat. You clearly have wisdom to have gathered such a fine collection." He waved his hand to indicate the multi-tiered library.

"I am a wise and just king," Nadiri replied. In truth, he was neither, but he was delusional, which was why Zion's attempt at distraction worked. "Very well. Let me know when it's time for me to do something." Zion just caught himself before he said, "Obviously."

The king turned and strode from the library, his guards falling into formation in front of and behind him. When the guards closed the door behind him, the sun returned, illuminating the library with its gentle, late-afternoon glow.

Mumbling about dead kings, the insanely high level of stupidity, and the short-sightedness of the current king, Zion continued his search.

Touching each book with his fingertips, he found the treasure he was looking for. It was hiding on the bottom shelf at the back of the fourth stack. He pulled it off the shelf with difficulty because of his bent and gnarled body. With the volume secured under his arm, he limped to the nearest table. Laying the book on the table, he ran his hand over the cover and felt a slight tingle. He had found it!

The book was old but well kept. Its cover had an ornate gold border around a picture of two swords. The one on the left was stunning. Ripples flowed up the blade to the cross guard with an angel in between it and the pommel, her arms and wings reaching toward the diamond pommel. A purple stone in her forehead caught and reflected the light. Zion didn't understand how a picture could do that.

As much as the sword on the left danced and sparkled, the one on the right swallowed the light. The only points of light on it were the two red stones in a demon's eyes on the hilt, its horns curling toward the black diamond pommel. Light Bringer and Light Taker indeed.

He opened the cover, the spine cracking in protest. Surprisingly, the first page contained a disclaimer:

> Be aware, seeker of this knowledge.
> It is not known if this work is complete or true.
> Proceed with caution.

Bah! Zion thought. He was a wizard of considerable strength and age. He could do what he wanted. All he had to do was cross-reference what he already knew with what the book said,

and he could extrapolate the missing pieces and decipher truth
from fiction. He turned to the next page, which was the table
of contents.

Table Of Contents

Zion started at the beginning, even though he was confident
he already knew what most of the book said. Three sentences
in, he was metaphorically knocked onto his butt. This book was
much more detailed than anything he had read before.

He was so engrossed in his reading that he didn't notice
Princess Luna watching from the opposite balcony, lying on her
belly as she peeked through the banister. She had seen the inter-
action between the wizard and her father and noted how the
wizard distracted her father so he wouldn't have to share any
information about the plan. Now that she knew which book
he was interested in, she crawled away from the railing and stole
through a secret door behind one of the bookshelves. She would
return later and read the book, so she could stay in the loop,
unbeknownst to Zion and her father. She would tell the servers
to fill their cups fuller than usual, which would buy her time
to study.

TWENTY-SEVEN

A ri had been mercilessly training Jaya, and as with everything else she'd seen him do, when it came to sword fighting, he was a natural. She taught him the basics of using a sword and was astonished when he instinctively integrated the Ballet of Breath with moves and combinations she had never seen before, which was no easy feat.

As they practiced, Light Bringer glowed in a myriad of colors in Jaya's hand. Ari was using Jaya's old sword.

"Yes! Use the sword's ladinya as a tool. Feel the flow of the vibration you choose." Raising her sword across her body, Ari blocked a slash. Then, pressing an advantage, she forced Jaya back a few steps. When he clued into her strategy, Light Bringer's blade burst with an orange light that almost blinded Sage, who was watching the training session from beside the fire where they were making breakfast.

"Channel the emotion into something positive!" Ari roared as the pace of their sparring hit another gear, their swords sparking with each block.

Light Bringer's blade changed to red. Grounding himself, Jaya gained the upper hand over Ari. When he thought he was triumphant, the light shifted to white. That was what Ari had been waiting for, the signal of a sneak attack. When Light Bringer flashed white light, she held up her left palm and absorbed it, pulling it into her body. Dropping her sword, she connected her wrists, palms facing Jaya, and released the transferred light as a sound wave. It struck the center of Jaya's chest, knocking him off his feet. He rolled with the momentum, then sprang to his feet in a fighting stance, Light Bringer glowing blood red.

Breathing hard, he looked up at Ari. "What the hell was that?" he asked, caught off guard by the move.

"What do you think it was?" Ari asked as she sheathed her sword and grabbed her water skin, uncorking the stopper.

Jaya slid Light Bringer home, the light dying out. "You fight dirty. That wasn't in the rules. We were using our swords."

"Close. Guess again." It was important that he figured it out on his own.

Jaya rested his left hand on Light Bringer, his fingers draped over the diamond in the pommel. The fingers of his right hand drummed his lower lip. Ari drank some water and wiped her brow while he thought.

"I got it! You're training me for real life, and in real life there are no rules. You weren't fighting dirty; you were using all your tools."

"That's exactly right. What else did I do?"

Jaya opened his mouth to say he didn't know, then he paused to replay the fight in his mind. By the time he reached the end, he understood. "You leveraged the situation. You didn't use any effort to 'create' ladinya. Instead, you took what I provided and turned it against me, knocked me down without expending any of your own ladinya. Highly efficient." Jaya was in awe. It was brilliant.

Ari winked at him. "Well done."

The three of them were sitting around the fire eating porridge with berries when Sage lifted their eyes and looked into the forest. "It's been close to ninety days since we met, just like last time. We've been all around, and now we're here." Sage's tone was light, not wanting to let the intruders know that they knew they were surrounded.

Ari nodded her understanding, then caught Jaya's gaze. For a moment he didn't understand. Then he realized Sage had spoken in code, indicating that ninety men were surrounding the camp.

He nodded to Ari. Then, acting naturally, he sent out his Senses, as Ari had taught him, and he knew exactly who was out there and where. He received the information just in time to thrust his hand in front of Ari's face, catching the arrow that was heading straight between her eyes.

"Thanks," Ari said as balls of yellow light appeared in her hands. She fired two hot yellow orbs into the forest, but she felt no satisfaction when a scream erupted between the two orbs as they found their targets. Nevertheless, the crossbows had been eliminated.

Jaya hadn't had a chance yet to use Light Bringer or his newly acquired skills. Whether that was a good or bad thing, he wasn't sure. Opening himself, he felt ladinya thunder through his body, penetrating every cell. It was glorious and intoxicating.

He stood and unsheathed Light Bringer, flooding the area in deep purple light. He corrected the flow of the channeled ladinya, sending it down the length of the sword and causing a rippling effect in red, orange, and yellow, the top half of the rainbow mimicking a merry fire. He was lit up and ready for the enemy, who was now just beyond the reach of his sword.

Stepping forward, he closed the gap and stabbed the first man through the heart. As he pulled the razor-sharp blade out of his victim's chest, he spun, cutting the man beside him in half, right through his diaphragm. Bowing, bending, and flowing, Jaya moved with their momentum, saving his energy by using what they were giving him. In a matter of minutes, he had dispatched his share of the threat.

Taking a deep breath, he sensed more men rushing out of the forest, trying to catch him off guard. Before he realized what he was doing, he reversed his grip on Light Bringer's hilt, "Bringer" pressing into his palm to remind him of his mission.

"Ari, Sage, down!" he bellowed, his voice tearing through the cacophony like a clarion over a battlefield. Ari dropped to her front, her cheek to the ground, before he finished the order.

Jaya shifted his grip and slammed his sword into the ground, bowing in supplication as a beam of ethereal light shot down from the heavens above. When it made contact with the diamond in the sword's pommel, a disk of prismatic light exploded across the battlefield, annihilating everything evil in its path. Men exploded, leaving behind pieces of their bodies for the birds, stopping the battle in the moment of stillness between an inhale and an exhale.

No one spoke or moved. The threat had been exterminated with extreme prejudice.

When Ari felt a faint hum ripple over her body, she lifted her head from where she was lying prone on the ground and searched for Jaya. What she saw made a tear of joy run down her cheek.

Jaya was bowing to Light Bringer, his hands gripping the handle. The area around him glowed as a celestial spotlight shone on him, illuminating the golden egg in which he was encased. The diamond in the pommel glowed with a brilliant white light, making the golden egg glisten, especially around Jaya's head, which made it look like he was wearing a crown of light. The purple stone in the angel's forehead pulsed, proclaiming she was a messenger sent by the higher power, sharing the news of an overdue arrival.

TWENTY-EIGHT

J aya was standing in front of a long rectangular table that had all nine seats filled. The high dome above the table emitted a soft light that illuminated the room. His silk robes hung from his shoulders to his sandaled feet. The robes were colorful with long sleeves that covered the backs of his hands. His strong, broad shoulders made him an imposing figure.

"You know you will lose all knowledge of this conversation and your knowledge from your time of study once you pass through the veil," the woman who was sitting in the center chair pointed out. She sat ramrod straight, her black hair swept into a messy bun on top of her head.

"Yes, Priscilla, I understand. However, I've built in the memory of this experience should I need it. It's one of the paths. I believe it's on page seven thousand three hundred and eighty-four of the contact, paragraph six, about halfway down the page. I know it's unorthodox, but as we know, this is an unorthodox situation."

The others all muttered in agreement.

"We are here to support you," Priscilla said. "And because you haven't been to Earth before, we're taking extra precautions in being particularly thorough."

"I understand and greatly appreciate it. I don't think I need to remind the council that should I fail, it will be the end of life here and there, as we know it, entering the void." He could tell by the looks on some of the council members' faces that they hadn't understood the severity of the threat until that moment.

"But we all know I can take some skills, gifts, and talents with me," Jaya said with a jovial tone. "And"—he rolled his hand comically—"I have contracts with others for help. Refer to the appendices for that information. We all know I have to try." He stood tall and proud, ready for his journey. He had known this time was coming. He had seen Apala put Light Taker into the vault and had spent all his time from that moment on learning about the magical sword and its twin, Light Bringer. He had even obtained Light Bringer, as a favor from Apala, to master and understand its magic. He had kept it for a few hundred years (or so he'd thought), becoming one with the sword as if it were his lover.

When he learned that Light Taker had been stolen by the Planter, to be triggered and put on Earth, he knew his thousands of years of study, observation, and planning had led to this moment.

"My birth will be unique, fulfilling events prophesying my coming," he explained. He had been working on this project, setting the shared contracts for over a thousand years. Some of those who had agreed to help him had been training on Earth for almost as long.

What the council didn't understand was that he would cross the veil with or without their approval, as he had no other choice.

"Jaya, we know you will cross the veil no matter what, so of course we will back you," Priscilla said. "Our job is to ensure success and to look at things from all angles to ensure your intention is clear and that you haven't bitten off more than you can chew." She raised her eyebrow as if to ask if Jaya understood. "We noticed you have much more detail for the pathways than is usually planned." She swept her hand over the seven leather-bound volumes in front of her. She had to sit up straight in her chair to see over them. "We don't encourage this degree of planning due to free will, but we are happy to make an exception due to the circumstances. The future of the light rests on your shoulders."

Jaya bowed his head in agreement. Then he looked up, his eyes filled with resolve. "We dare not delay any longer. It is time."

With that, Priscilla, the head councilwoman, stamped his contract with a gold seal, approving the life journey. The runner standing behind her chair loaded the seven leather-bound volumes onto a cart. It was no small feat, as each volume was three inches thick, almost a foot long, and just as wide. Pushing the cart to the door, he closed it behind him. He was taking it directly to the records room, to be filed properly for future reference.

"I speak on behalf of the council when I say good luck and have fun. Be the light," she said with a mischievous sparkle in her eye. Everyone in the room chuckled at the inside joke.

"Thank you, everyone." Jaya replied, bowing his head and holding his hands over his heart in gratitude.

Turning from his friends' smiling faces, he strode from the room, going directly to the transition center. It was controlled chaos, like rush hour at a train station, bustling with souls who were looking for the correct doorway to transition from the Otherside to Earth through the veil.

Jaya stood against the wall for a moment, absorbing the party-like atmosphere of souls bumping into each other and laughing over shared experiences as they made their way to their correct destinations. He glanced at a doorway labeled "Helpers' Lane" and saw people talking and making agreements. Then they would go to the desk, and the clerk would take the agreement amendment form to be added to both contracts. Unlike those souls who were still looking for help, he had planned everything. He had a specific goal that had allowed him to plan much more than a soul normally would.

He was about to turn to a nondescript door hidden in the corner when he heard his name being called by a familiar voice. He turned and saw his best friend, John.

"Are you finally making the trip?" John asked, clapping Jaya on the shoulder.

"Yep! It's time," Jaya replied, pulling John into a hug.

"I guess that's a good thing?" John wasn't sure which view Jaya was taking.

Jaya nodded. "Sure is."

"Well, they're in good hands with you," John replied.

"Thank you. Are you heading down? How many lives now? What are you focusing on?" Jaya was excited to have a quick catch-up with his friend no matter how brief.

"I am. This will be life journey number ninety. And I'm looking for a level-ten forgiveness."

Jaya sucked in air. That was one of the biggest life challenges to experience. Only the strongest souls even tried forgiveness, let alone a level ten. But if anyone could do it, it was John.

"Have you seen Nathanial or Ruby?" John asked. "I've been looking for them." The four of them were very close.

"They went down a while ago," Jaya said. John didn't ask any further questions, as it was considered rude to ask about others' life journeys.

"Maybe I'll run into them. Good luck, my friend. I won't be there to help you this time, but maybe our paths will cross." They embraced and then John made his way to Helpers' Lane, Jaya passing through a side door.

He climbed the winding staircase in meditation, preparing. At the top, it opened to a round room lit by a gentle light shining from the white stone walls. He sat in the middle of the white plush rug that covered the floor in the center of the room. To transition, he needed to focus or else he would miss the doorway and his opportunity. If he didn't do things perfectly, he wouldn't bring what he needed with him, and it would all be for naught.

Sitting cross-legged, he took a deep breath, followed by another and another. When he was clear, he slowed the ladinya flow, compressing it and his beingness. The light that was his body dimmed and condensed. When he felt the sweet spot, he brought his focus to the faceted wall that appeared in front of him. The portal shimmered with rainbows, blocking his view of what was on the other side. He watched the wall patiently, knowing the time was coming.

Sooner than he expected, black rippled over the wall, diminishing the light and creating a gateway between the Otherside and Earth. He stood and walked right through the wall without hesitation. Compressing his ladinya further, he became an ember of light, floating on a moonbeam, looking at two lovers in bed.

Twenty-Nine

Before Ari could take another breath, the brilliant light died, leaving the reality of the holocaust in front of her.

Lifting his head, Jaya looked around him, ready to jump back into the battle, then he shrank back in horror. Outside the charred circle of earth was a ring of obliterated bodies, made by Light Bringer. Beyond that ring a tangle of dead bodies covered the forest floor. A number of them had been sliced in half.

All the men who had made Ari their target had been incinerated to some degree. Jaya would have had a hard time counting how many men had attacked Ari because so little was left of their bodies. The red mist her attack had created was still settling around her. Jaya hadn't realized how dangerous she could be, and he was horrified. She was a killer. But he was too. Looking around, he realized it was the amount of gore that made him upset. What a waste of human life, all by their choice. He had merely facilitated the accumulation of every decision these men had ever made by helping them conclude the last one. He would not claim guilt because of their choices.

Ari turned around, and Jaya had to look closer to see the splattered viscera on her glistening, blood-red bodysuit. It was just like the second day they were together, although she had been wearing her traveling garb that time.

Having pondered that lovely thought, he shifted his focus to Sage. They were standing at the edge of a pit that hadn't been there a few minutes earlier. It had ten men in it. Looking down at the men, he realized they were soldiers.

"What do we have here?" Ari asked Sage as she joined them.

"A group of talkative men," Sage replied with a sneer.

"We ain't tellin' you no-fing," a taller one spat, his bald head reflecting Light Bringer's purple glow.

"Uh-huh," Ari replied as if she'd heard that a million times. "Who sent you?" she asked as if she were asking the lead brute if he'd like sugar in his tea.

The soldier tried to spit on her but failed miserably, making a fool of himself, spittle dribbling down his chin.

"I'm going to be honest with you," Ari said. "We've been working and traveling hard, and frankly, we need to move on. Is there any chance you can give us the answers we seek, so we can be on our way?" Ari would give them one chance to choose a different path. If they didn't, she would show them the path to life everlasting.

"You're just going to kill us anyway," the soldier said, his comrades nodding in agreement.

"Not at all. If you choose a different path, we will gladly let you go. If not, you will die here." She said it as a fact of life, not an ultimatum. "Do any of you want to answer my questions?"

"King Nadiri of the Eighth Kingdom will prevail whether you kill us or not," a soldier with a missing front tooth and a long, greasy ponytail said. "You might as well kill us now."

"Do you choose a path of taking the lives of innocents?"

"We take what we want and kill who we want, and we aren't going to change!" the soldier yelled. His companions cheered in agreement. Apparently, they all thought she was bluffing.

"Do you speak as a group?" she asked, making eye contact with each one of them.

"Yes," they all muttered.

"So be it. This is your choice." Turning from the pit, she

nodded at Sage, who nodded solemnly in reply. Sage moved the earth and filled the pit, burying the men alive. Their screams were only heard for a moment.

THIRTY

They hiked through the forest with surprising ease, Sage leading and Ari teaching.

"It's time to learn about the houses," Ari said to Jaya as they climbed over a fallen log, the carnage an hour behind them. "Do you remember what I said about them?"

Jaya thought for a moment. "The houses are centers of ladinya in the human body, each one corresponding to a color, organs, characteristics, challenges, and lessons."

"That's exactly right!" Sage could hear the excitement in Ari's voice at having a smart, willing student.

"Oh, and seven is the highest number," Jaya added. "For a human."

"Right again." Ari was impressed. He was a quick learner. "One of the advantages to being Light Born or Star Born like you is that we can work through the houses in a conscious way, opening doors and dimensions because we are increasing our frequency in a way that 'normal' humans can't. Light Borns can only move on to the next house once they've mastered the lessons of the previous one. Light Borns start in the first house, and Star Borns"—she pointed at Jaya, making sure he knew she was talking about him—"pull their light from above and, therefore, start in the seventh house and work their way down."

"Why is that?" Jaya asked.

"Because you came here through unconventional means with crystal-clear intention. You are certain of your purpose, and now you have to 'work'—I use the term loosely—at grounding every-thing in this physical plane, starting at the top, or the seventh house, and working your way down."

Jaya nodded in understanding. "You said only Light Borns have houses. So, Sage doesn't have them?" He wanted to make sure he covered every point.

"No. Every human has houses, but only Light Borns and Star Borns can leverage them to allow us to move through dimensions or increase our natural gifts. Because we have the special talent of working with ladinya, we aspire to be intentional with our learning, so we can grow and be of service. We spend our lives working to master that ability and to use it in different ways, branching out from our natural tendencies and talents. Each level has criteria to master before advancing. The higher the number, the more learned and experienced you are considered to be. Obviously, it's the opposite for you. Also, Sage is extraordinary because she is an Earth Walker and has special magic of her own." Ari smiled at Sage over her shoulder.

"Light Borns start in the first house, located at the bottom of the spine. The first house is supported by your family or tribe, knowing and understanding where you came from and being rooted to the earth physically when you sit down. This is impor-tant because light workers need to know how to ground their energy to prevent accidents, including accidental death. We learn to throw or send ladinya through our earth connection if it's getting out of control instead of blowing ourselves or others up. This is why being supported by a tribe or a family is important. If an untrained Light Born is in a situation where they may be a danger to themselves or others, a member of the tribe whom they trust can talk them down or convince the danger to pass the light to Mother Earth, who will gladly take it."

Ari held up her hand to halt his next question. "Star Borns

start in the seventh house, open to the higher power, whatever that means to you, and connection to ladinya."

"If I haven't moved through all the houses, how will I ever be able to use Light Bringer to its full potential?" Jaya asked.

"You won't, but you don't need to. Being Star Born, you already have the clarity built in. You just need to learn how to keep everything open through the Ballet of Breath. And I'm here to help you when you need it. You just have to walk your path, and everything will be OK. It's a lifelong journey for everyone. I've been at it for almost nine hundred and fifty years. Having said that, you are Star Born, so the rules are a little different for you."

Jaya gulped.

"Light born are long-lived," Ari said, as if Jaya hadn't figured that part out yet.

"You said every house has a color," Jaya said as they walked through a stream.

"What are they?"

"The first house is red, and the second is orange. The third is yellow, and the fourth is green, although I use pink when I'm healing. The fifth is blue, the sixth is purple, and the seventh is white."

"Like a rainbow," Jaya said in awe.

Ari laughed. "Yes, just like a rainbow. I was wondering how long it would take you to connect the dots."

"Wait a second. That's what's on my scabbard." Jaya grabbed his sword, shuffling his steps, so he could look at it and walk at the same time.

He looked up at Ari, who could see the gears turning in his head. "Light Bringer," he said in awe. Then a look of dismay crossed his face. He stopped walking and stood in the center of the path. Ari and Sage stopped, too, Sage using the opportunity to take a drink of water from the skin hanging at their side.

"Light is supposed to move freely through our bodies, the houses, so we can light the way, the Ballet of Breath being a method to keep the way clear, but when it's not, ladinya gets…"

"Stuck, blocked, stopped, obstructed," Ari said.

"And causes dis-ease, which can manifest in uncountable ways." Standing crookedly, as if the weight of what he was processing was too heavy a burden, his eyes glazed over, and he mumbled to himself. Drool dripped out of the corner of his mouth as his mind raced, reminding Ari of another time long ago when he'd had a drop of drool dripping from his mouth. If she hadn't understood how much information he was processing, she would have thought he was a degenerate.

"I have to bring the light… to the darkness," he said, snapping out of his trance. "Keeping the houses open. I can do that." He didn't say the last sentence with much conviction.

"Ari," he said, looking at his protector, mentor, and guide, "why do we do this? What's the point? What's the purpose of all this work?"

"And therein lies the question. Although the answer is different for every person, the seed of that answer is the same. To grow, learn, experience, and create that which has never been before." She was teaching him things that took most Light Borns hundreds of years to wrap their heads around, and he was being forced to do it in days, if not minutes. But he was succeeding, and that was all that mattered.

"Learn? Learn what?" Jaya asked.

"It depends on the person and what they want to learn or experience on their life journey. Some beings choose to experience forgiveness. Others choose independence. That's a whole different conversation. It's been said that some come for a very special reason, like you did." Her eyes bored into him.

"Like I did? Geez." He barely stopped himself from rolling his eyes.

"You came here with purpose. Unlike everyone else, your birth was foretold thousands of years ago, and when the stars aligned..." Ari chuckled to herself at an inside joke. "...you came to fulfill your destiny."

"Coming here was a choice?" Jaya whispered, his voice filled with wonder.

Ari nodded. "A choice you made."

At that moment, Ari saw something click in Jaya, followed by a ripple through the ether. He squared his shoulders with renewed confidence.

"I had to come. I've been studying Light Taker and Light Bringer since their inception, and I'm the only one who has any chance to stop them. And, apparently, there were contracts to fulfill."

Ari and Sage looked at Jaya, then each other, then back at Jaya.

"What?" Ari asked, astounded.

"I had a vision back there. Well, apparently it was a memory. Whatever it was, it unlocked my knowledge. With everything that was going on, I forgot, but you must have just triggered my memory. I can access everything now."

"Everything?" Ari asked in disbelief.

Jaya nodded without hesitation. "Everything."

"Contracts? Life purpose?" Ari asked.

"All of it," Jaya replied. "By the way, you're both doing an awesome job. Thanks for showing up."

"Well, that's amazing!" Ari couldn't wait to hear about it, if he was willing to share. But apparently, that was a story for another time.

"Why didn't I remember it before?" he asked. "Like, when I was a child or any time before today?"

"What fun would that be?" Ari exclaimed. "One reason why life is amazing is that we don't know everything. You wouldn't want to have hindsight in the present moment, knowing where your choices took you before you made them."

"At least I would know if we succeeded or not," he muttered.

"Jaya, listen to me. You *chose* to come here to save humanity. There's great power in that. And with that choice you took gifts and talents that would equip you for success. You also have me and Sage to help. It will be OK. Think of it that way."

Jaya looked over Ari's shoulder at Sage, who nodded in agreement.

Ari held her hands up, palms to the sky, mimicking a scale. "Worst-case scenario, you try your best and fail miserably by dying, thereby plunging humanity into darkness until the end of time. Yes, it's horrible, but you won't care much cause you'll be dead."

Ari moved one palm down and the other up, throwing the scales off balance. "Best-case scenario, you do exactly what you need to and save us all. It's all up to you. No pressure, by the way." She smiled sideways at him, then dropped her hands and continued down the path.

THIRTY-ONE

They walked in silence for a time, Jaya absorbing what Ari had said and processing all the new memories and information. These were ancient teachings, and she was still only telling him the first level. To understand the rest, she needed to establish a solid foundation of understanding and trust in Jaya, or it would all be for naught, and then they would be in real trouble.

Sage stopped and turned. "We are fast approaching the Tough Plains. I'm told we have someone waiting for us. Actually, a lot of someones. An army." Sage sounded dismayed, stress seeping from their voice.

"Let's go see who it is." Ari already had a pretty good idea and hoped they would be able to sort it out peacefully. It was a slim possibility, but a girl could dream.

They stepped out of the forest into a clearing that was a league wide and a league long. It was flat, covered with long grass that was brown but on the verge of waking from its winter slumber. To their left was a sheer rock wall with a façade of sandy brown layers. The vertical wall reached into the clouds, making it impossible to guess the height of the peak. On their right, on the other side of the meadow, was a cliff that dropped into a canyon. From where they were standing, they could barely see the other side. If any of them fell off, there would be no chance of survival. The canyon floor was hundreds of feet below.

Jaya had just finished taking in the scenery when something

on the other side of the clearing caught his eye. He loosened his Senses, and as soon as he did, he felt a searing pain through his skull that brought him to his knees.

"Jaya! What happened?" Ari exclaimed, kneeling beside him and putting her arm over his shoulders.

Breathing hard, he pointed. Ari looked that way and saw figures in the trees. She stood up and started humming "ohm" to bring in the light and immediately fell to her knees beside Jaya. She took a few deep breaths to process what had happened.

"OK, someone on the other side has cast a light net that is preventing us from using our gifts." She nodded to Jaya. "I know who it is and what's going on."

She stood up and walked forward, projecting her voice. "Zion! Zion! I know you're there. Come out before I come over there and drag you out, you weasel!"

Ari was starting to get annoyed.

"How are you going to win this battle if you don't have your powers?" a sleazy voice asked from the other side of the clearing behind the trees. "Just give me the boy, and we'll be on our way."

"Give you the boy? What are you talking about? He's just someone who's traveling with us for protection. Why would you want this person who's irrelevant to anything going on right now?"

"You know, Ariella, for someone who supposedly values truth above all else, you're really good at lying. Is it a character flaw? It must be. What else could it be?"

Ari knew exactly what he was talking about, and she actually agreed with him. How could she lie and kill and think it was acceptable? She concluded that her actions were always backed with the intention of the higher good. Because in some circumstances, death was the best option, for there were way worse things than dying. She didn't have enough information about their current situation to make informed decisions, so she relied on her intuition and being of service. If saving potentially millions of souls meant she needed to tell a lie once in a while, she still had peace in her heart.

"Him and Light Bringer will be mine one way or the other. Now enough of this. Hand him over," the voice crackled, sending a shiver down Sage's spine.

Unknowingly, Zion had answered a few of Ari's questions. It had been him all along, and he was using King Nadiri and Light Taker as pawns for his plan, though what his plan was, she didn't know.

"Why are you doing this? You can walk away and live a quiet, peaceful life." Ari figured if she had Zion's attention, she should take advantage of it.

"I can only do that with you by my side, and you've made it clear that's not what you want, so I'll have what I want." His anger was so intense that Ari, Sage, and Jaya could feel the compressive wave as it swept across the plain.

"I can't change the way I feel, and I have always been truthful with you," Ari said. "Hear me now. If you continue on this path, it won't end well for you. I guarantee it. Maybe not today, but this will be the end of you. You can still walk a different path. It's not too late." Zion had never moved beyond the third house. Therefore, he had never learned how to give or receive love. He was all about hate and greed and would stop at nothing to have his self-loathing satisfied to boost his ego, no matter who got in the way.

"Oh, and who's going to stop me? You? Don't be ridiculous. Last chance—hand over the boy!" Zion sent a shock of lightning through the air, scorching everyone who was standing too close before it dissipated.

"Over my dead body!" Ari shouted, her clothes shifting to a blood-red bodysuit. Long daggers appeared between her fingers, and she held their hilts in her palms. She backed up behind Sage, motioning for Jaya to stand behind her.

"Sage, do your thing. Jaya, stay as close to Sage as possible. I don't want to leave you, but I have to take this opportunity to take out Zion. I'll ride the wave and take out as many as I can on my way to him. Show no mercy." Sage nodded in understanding, their chin held high.

There was a crack, and a light dome appeared over them. A sparkling golden light covered the entire plain. As long as the light dome was up they would be cut off from their powers and help, should any come. Ari wasn't counting on it. The only way to destroy a light dome was to kill its creator. Ari could see through it and noticed a storm was brewing, the air becoming heavy with ozone.

Looking at the sky, Ari saw clouds collecting and swirling overhead. Thunder rocked the plain as she turned her attention back to the men on horses coming out of the forest. The ones up front looked like hardened warriors who had been born and baptized on the battlefield. When they formed up, Ari counted roughly a thousand men and a few hundred horses. She was glad they were almost evenly matched, the conditions favoring Ari, Jaya, and Sage, of course.

Sage knelt down, putting their palms flat on the ground and bending their fingers to establish the connection that was their birthright. Closing their eyes, Sage focused on the damp dirt, offering their energy in exchange for connection. Singing a dirge as old as Mother Earth herself, Sage pulsed their hands, creating ripples. At first only the smallest pebbles shook grudgingly, then as Sage fed more intention into the ground, engaging their arms and shoulders in an up-and-down motion and then using their whole upper body, tiny ripples appeared. As Sage continued to move in time with the dirge, the ground rippled toward the army. Sage was the proverbial pebble in the pond.

Using the potential energy the ground held, Sage drew on the power, increasing the size and frequency of the wave. Dirt filled the air, creating a cloud of dust as the waves became taller than Ari. Sweat dripped from Sage's brow as they stood, using their whole body to pulse the ground.

The tsunami of dirt, grass, and rock cascaded toward the oncoming army, throwing the cavalry into the air at the peak of the wave. The screams of horses mixed with the screaming men who were tossed from their saddles, many landing under their horses.

Ari ran along the top of the last wave as it surged toward the oncoming army. Right before the wave washed over them, she launched herself through the air, spinning and twisting. While in the air, she shifted her bodysuit from blood-red into a thing of nightmares. Crossing her arms over her chest, a cape flew out, whipping as if in a hurricane. Razor-sharp blades sprouted from the fabric, shredding everything in its path.

While Ari was controlling the cape as a second fighting entity, matching blades sprang from her legs, back, and forearms, contributing to the carnage. Pulling the blades back in as she landed, she used the momentum to cartwheel over the next horde of men who rushed toward her. Again, she used her suit to inflict maximum damage, and she was not disappointed.

The air was full of red mist, the clamor of armor, and the screams of dying men. Through her Senses, Ari received infinite amounts of information that she used to make decisions at the speed of light, turning her into a killing machine.

With blades in both hands, she ducked left, pulling them across the abdomen of the first man as he swung his sword past her head. Using him as a launching point, she leapt off his back and dove deeper into the fray, hacking and slashing with perfect efficiency as she cartwheeled past the men. She showed no mercy.

She fought and killed man after man. It was kill or be killed.

The longer they fought, the more tumultuous the sky became. Heavy, dark gray clouds formed over their heads, blocking out the sunlight. Thunder boomed, and the air within the dome became damp and heavy. Ari realized she was being pushed toward the edge of the cliff and knew to be careful not to get too close, realizing this was Zion's plan.

Turning to her right, she steered her attacker so they were moving parallel to the ledge. Out of the corner of her eye, she saw a man charging toward her, and she was forced to take a few steps sideways, closer to the edge. The storm clouds had built and were ready to burst when she looked over the shoulder of the man attacking her. At that moment, time slowed.

She saw Jaya across the plain, fighting for his life, a normal sword in his hand making him no less deadly, when a faint movement in the sky through the top of the light dome caught her attention. Bursting through the dark cloud cover were the silhouettes of great winged beasts. They were huge, silver-blue winged warhorses with glittering silver horns spiraling from their foreheads. Their silver breast plates reflected the blinding light in the building thunderstorm. Riding them were armored war maidens clad in metal corsets, leather skirts, and knee-high armor-plated boots. Their long hair flowed behind them from under their faceless helmets as they dived toward the dome. Each was unique in her beauty, but they could all have been sisters. Across their backs were swords. Each held a spear in one hand and a bow in the other, full quivers strapped to their saddles.

The commander, as indicated by the gleaming wings on the sides of her helmet, threw her spear with godly speed into the light dome. It sailed through the light and shattered the dome, motes of light dancing on the wind for a moment. When the dome disappeared, Ari knew for certain that her sisters in arms, the Valkyries, had arrived.

Ari heard their terrifying battle cry as they joined the conflict. As their screams pierced the air, all movement on the battlefield stopped, the soldiers turning their attention to the sky. Before they could acknowledge who had come, the Valkyries plowed into the fray, their warhorses trampling soldiers who couldn't get out of the way in time.

With the dissolution of the light dome, Ari felt her power ignite in her belly. Stepping closer to the edge of the cliff, she dispatched a charging soldier by using his momentum to disembowel him. When he was taken out, she turned her attention to Jaya just as a black bolt of lightning grounded so close to his back that she was surprised his shirt didn't ignite. As she slammed her knife into the eye of the man in front of her, she saw Zion jump onto Jaya's back. It was no easy feat, considering Jaya had also felt the light dome fall and had pulled Light Bringer half out of its scabbard. Zion locked his arms around Jaya's neck, almost choking him and pulling him off balance. Ari sparked the embers of dangerous red light in her right palm. As always, she channeled emotion as the fuel for the light, this time focusing on the hatred she had for these people who hurt innocents, and her fear of failing. With her left hand, she pulled her blades through the latest attacker's neck. His head tumbled to the ground, blood spurting into her face as his body fell. She didn't notice, though, her attention on Zion as he wrapped his legs around Jaya, still clinging to his back.

Ari brought her arm up. Seeing the perfect shot across the battlefield, she let a deadly fireball fly. It streaked past fighting men and women, through gaps that only existed for a millisecond. Before it reached its intended target, Zion pulled every ounce of energy from the ether and ignited it with a spark. It created a plasma lightning bolt that disappeared with Jaya and Light Bringer, leaving a circle of charred earth behind.

Traveling using lightning was not common. In fact, Zion was the only person whom Ari knew that could do it. While growing up together, he had explained how he did it. She knew it required phenomenal amounts of energy for just one person to use lightning as a means of travel, so she couldn't fathom the amount of energy needed to transport two people that way. She didn't think it was possible because the amount of energy flowing through a normal body would cause it to incinerate. The only way it was possible was that Jaya was Star Born, which meant his body was able to handle the extreme heat.

She had just enough time for the thought to form before the ether folded in on itself, air rushing in to fill the space too quickly and making it explode in a concussion of planetary proportions that blew across the battlefield. It struck Ari in her diaphragm, flinging her off the ledge and into the canyon. As she plummeted through the air, the wind knocked out of her, time seemed to be suspended, allowing her to reflect on her life.

"I don't understand," Ari said.

"What's the mantra?"

"Ugh." Ari rolled her eyes.

"This is why you don't succeed. You've always been closed-minded, which is the opposite of what you need to be. Therefore, you will never grow, expand, or engage in the power that is knowledge. You have the power, being Light Born, but you'll never get to where you want to go." Apala's voice had an edge and a tenderness to it.

Ari took a deep breath and felt something loosen deep in her belly. She closed her eyes, moving her feet shoulder-width apart, her arms at her sides and her palms open in supplication. Exhaling, she focused on moving the energy and pulling it all together, so she could use her breath to cleanse it. She breathed in, contracting her core and forcing the ball to condense. With the pause at the apex of the inhale, she used the energy she created with the air she breathed to hook into the ball in her belly, pulling it in until the two became one. When the process was complete, she contracted her core further while constricting her lungs. Out of her mouth, the air and the ladinya rode out of the bottom of her lungs to the top. Her next inhale had hope, growth, and groundedness, and Ari drank it in like water. She opened her hazel eyes, meeting Apala's gaze.

"Oh, my child. You are going places." Apala said, but Ari barely understood her mentor. She was laughing, crying, and trying to talk all at once.

"What was that?" Ari was happy and light, feeling a gentle hum in the depth of her belly. She drank it in.

"That was your attitude shift." Apala chuckled to herself as she wiped tears from her eyes. "I've seen a lot of energy moving by you humans, but I don't think I've ever seen something like that, especially by someone so young. You're a natural."

Ari considered that memory the real start of her journey. By choosing to open her second house when she was only in her mid-two hundreds, she knew she was destined to walk a great path. She had always tried her hardest, doing the right things, and she was ashamed she had failed despite her centuries of hard work and dedication. She had cherished every minute of her life, the good, the bad, and the ugly. Her only regret was that she had let Jaya down. She had let everyone down.

Just as that note of remorse settled in her heart, they caught her.

ABOUT THE AUTHOR

Ashley LeBlanc is an Emotion Code and Body Code practitioner and has been working as a holistic health care practitioner for ten years. A veteran of the Canadian Navy, she began her holistic health journey after early release from service due to a diagnosis of mal de debarquement syndrome, a debilitating illness that causes daily seasickness on land. It wasn't until discovering techniques that affect energy in the body leading to rewiring the brain that she found full healing and a new career path unfold. Today, Ashley's holistic training supports people in removing the interference in their subconscious the same way it was removed for her—allowing their bodies to heal themselves and finally live the life they want. Through her *A Soldier of Light Novels*, she hopes to share many of the incredible natural body energy principles she learned during her journey.

Ashley lives in Victoria, BC, where she operates OM Wellness Victoria. *The Chosen One - A Soldier of Light Novel, Book One* is her first novel.

Printed in the USA
CPSIA information can be obtained
at www.ICGtesting.com
JSHW021928050724
65792JS00004B/7/J